THE FINK

A LANCE GEDRIN MYSTERY

GREG
GOUNTANIS

RB
ROWDY BOOKS

Published by Rowdy Books

Ebook ISBN: 978-1-953762-03-0

Paperback ISBN: 978-1-953762-01-6

Cover design by Deranged Doctor Design

First edition: November 2020

THE LANCE GEDRIN SERIES

The Night Contract (Lance Gedrin #1)

The Fink (Lance Gedrin #2)

The Loran (Lance Gedrin #3)

The Jobber (Lance Gedrin #4)

The Lance Gedrin Box Set (Books 1-4)

1

Henri made friends with the monkeys. He stood at attention like a Navy SEAL at roll call and got down on all fours. He whined and rolled on his back. He stuck his tongue out. If Henri were getting graded, he'd pass with flying colors. Know thy audience. Play to the crowd. The monkeys were fans. Plain and simple. They cheered and tapped their craniums.

Henri held his right paw up like a flamingo and looked back at me. I nodded and gave him more leash. I was a chill fur padre, and Henri had a service pass. Not many Dobermans could say their old owner was a serial killer and their new owner gave people concussions for breakfast. Legally. But truth is stranger than fiction sometimes. And laughing is the best game in town. Henri and I were Laurel and Hardy without the monochrome. We went with the flow till the flow had other plans.

Henri licked the glass, and the monkeys made farting noises from their side of things. The Oregon Zoo had hundreds of exhibits, but Henri was on a mission. He pawed at the glass and barked twice. The monkeys cheered. Two minutes later the show fizzled out, and Henri bid adieu. We trudged on no worse for the wear.

I looked at the zoo directory and Henri licked all the passersby. I didn't have a game plan, but I had three choices. Curtain 1: See every exhibit in the place. Start at point A and make it all the way to point Z. Curtain 2: Close my eyes and wherever my pinkie taketh me I shall go. Curtain 3: See the best damned exhibit. Quality over quantity. I racked my brain long and hard, and decided.

Quality.

I smiled and hung a left at the fork in the path. Freedom was muy bueno. When you spend twelve years in a box for a murder you didn't commit and come seconds away from getting a three-drug cocktail that will stop your heart forever, you appreciate choices. Both big and small. Clean air, too.

And in a few hours, I'd be on a plane back to business. I'd be in Sin City with one simple task: kick Nik Juko's ass. He was a punk, but he was also the number-one contender for the heavyweight title. On paper, anyway. My agent, Mark Sims, couldn't get me the big fight after my Chicago legal woes, but he got me the next best thing: a number-one contender fight in forty-eight hours. Beat Juko, get my title shot. Lose to Juko...and I'd be delivering gluten-free pizzas somewhere.

After I kicked Juko's ass, the plan was to make it to Horse-shoe Bend. Numero tres on my ever-expanding bucket list. As much as I enjoyed beating people's brains in, I was a nomad. And a nomad couldn't rest on his laurels or play house. Evolve. Live. Learn.

That's the way to do it, hombre.

I walked past three very boring exhibits, two boring exhibits, and one slightly less boring exhibit. Then I found it.

The African painted dog. One of the best creatures in the whole damned zoo.

But the people by the exhibit were paying no attention to the painted dog. They were mobbed around something else, and I heard a frightened gasp.

Then the crowd broke for a second and I saw a man lying in a pool of blood.

2

I expected nothing less. Chaos followed me like that ole rabbit at the Greyhound track. I was just six weeks removed from my last bout with death and destruction, but records are meant to be broken. I made my way up to the crowd. Henri pulled on his leash. Man's best friend should be dubbed man's best body whisperer. Henri had known the score before I'd even laid eyes on the gawkers. The sea parted for us. And when I pushed my way to the front, I realized I was right back in the thick of things.

Because I was joined at the hip with the man on the ground.

He was my cutman.

Maximo Bentini had hung around boxing gyms since he was seven years old. He'd tag along and do his dad's wraps as the old man rose up the amateur ranks and then the pro ranks. Old Man Bentini had a springy uppercut that never went out of style, and Young Bentini would step in the ring and trade jabs with me and all the other aficionados. He really just wanted to get closer to his old man. Bentini loved the fight game, but no matter how you sliced it, the genetics had skipped a generation. So when a brutal knockout later ended the old man's career, Bentini used his brain and found a better way to stay in the game. He sat in the corner and tended to cuts, scrapes, bruises, and pricks. The fighters called him "Fast Stitch." *Suck it up and he'll fix that cut.*

Bentini had found his calling. Every camp wanted him for every title fight. They flashed slimy brown envelopes and sent secret admirers to his place. But Bentini never forgot his roots. It had all started with his old man at Sal's gym, and so that's where he stayed. And that's how Bentini joined my corner as a cutman, putting all his munchkins through college. Then I lost my liberty, and he quit the game. I heard he was selling international SIM cards for a stretch. Then he went off the grid.

Till Sims found him and put him back on payroll for the Juko fight.

Some good that did.

Bentini was lying on his side, clutching his rib cage. Blood pooled out like sangria. A Good Samaritan held his hand as the clock ticked for the EMTs. I knelt down beside him, and Bentini recognized me in a heartbeat. He smiled, his face losing color, and gritted his teeth like he was fighting Father Time. Which he was.

I stepped in, and the Good Samaritan stepped out.

"Long-ass time," Bentini said. The words gargled with blood.

"Hell yeah, brother."

I held his hand and waited. Henri licked his forehead. A few more minutes and he'd be a goner. I'd gotten my medical degree from the school of hard knocks. I'd seen *Homo sapiens* spill their last breath on the ring turnbuckle, on the Pontiac

Correctional shitter, and on luxury high-rise bedding. Bentini would add "zoo" to my resume soon.

He looked up at me, then down at his right pocket. He did it three more times. Back and forth like a yo-yo till I finally got it. I looked at his pocket. A small piece of paper stuck out like a sore thumb. I hesitated for a second, then I grabbed it just as the EMTs arrived. They pushed me away and went to work. They hoisted him onto a stretcher and took him away. Bentini nodded at me on the way out. He didn't give a thumbs-up, but you can't have your cake and eat it too.

As the crowd petered out, and Henri circled me with the leash, I looked at the piece of paper in my hand. I examined it from every angle and knew right then that my comeback fight had a subplot.

It was a short note. Only three words.

It read, "2 Seconds Left."

3

The devil's in the details. To the untrained eye, the note was simple. A clock tells time and seconds make up units of time. Two seconds left. A countdown to something special. But to the discerning eye, seconds were slang. They were the lingo for a niche audience. Put "two" in front of it all and you get a threat clear as day.

Seconds were boxing cornermen.

Most fighters had three: a cutman, an assistant trainer, and a head trainer. The seconds held you together between rounds. They shouted and cajoled and grimaced and grunted and took all the credit in victory and all the shit in defeat. They threw in the towel when it looked like you'd croak in the ring, and they kept the cameras far away when the moment was right. To sum it all up and put a bow on it, they were family, friend, and foe. At all times. They were the team of all teams, and no fighter ever won without them.

One hell of a note.

The messenger was mowing down my cornermen.

The cutman first.

Two seconds left.

All on the eve of my weigh-in.

I racked my brain for the culprit. My list of less-than-amicable interactions was longer than the neck of the giraffe we passed after the monkeys. Maybe it was the Greyhound driver from Idaho, or the bartender at the local watering hole, or the flesh-eating Zemun hombres from Chicago. I started with my most recent disagreements and worked my way back. The Zemun stood out for obvious reasons, but that was too easy. The honchos were still no bail pending trial, and I doubted they had any infrastructure in the northeast after I was through with them. Plus, Bentini's body had no special markings. No tats. No animal bites. No tooth marks. I looked at Henri, and he didn't make any suggestions, so I went through more possibilities in my head. I went all the way back to pre-Pontiac, analyzing and critiquing each entry in my brain. I stood there for three minutes and would have stood there for three more, if it wasn't for the Great Dane that attacked me.

He slobbered all over my left kneecap, then rested both his paws on my tibia.

The owner said, "Bruce is so clumsy. Sorry about that."

I didn't mind the big boy's etiquette because (a) Henri's manners weren't much better, and (b) his owner would have made Elizabeth Hurley jealous in her prime. She tucked her black curls behind her ears, and when she flashed her pearly whites her cheeks had dimples on both sides. I was smitten from jump street, but I didn't tip my hand.

"No problemo," I said.

She tugged at the big boy's leash and got him off me. "It's nice that I'm not the only one dependent on a furry monstrosity in a place like this."

"I got Henri in easy-peasy."

"No wait?"

8

"Nada."

The owner laughed and scratched Henri's whiskers. He was in doggy heaven.

"Must have a ginormous infirmity to bypass the red tape," she said. "I'm team scoliosis."

"My mind is a super-fragile organ that plays no favorites," I replied.

She looked puzzled for a second, then held out her hand. "Tanya Mimi. Nice to meet you, Morpheus."

I never shake strangers' hands at the zoo. Maybe it's the learned fear of being shanked or the possibility of a surface pathogen getting its revenge. The monkeys can't be trusted. But for Mimi, I wanted to break the rules. Fervor had no equal.

I shook her hand.

"Lance Gedrin. Pleasure meeting you, lion tamer."

Mimi smiled and walked away with Bruce. She had a skip to her step and twirled the leash like it was a sparkly baton.

I decided right then and there that Henri needed more socialization. And I did too.

We caught up to Mimi and Bruce.

"Do you always stalk strangers at the zoo?" Mimi said.

"I—"

"Messing with you, dude. You're funny." She stopped, and Henri and Bruce inspected each other.

"The moment of truth," I said.

Mimi looked at the canine soiree and nodded. "One time Bruce grabbed a stick and poked a chihuahua with it, but this looks much more promising."

She was right. Bruce licked Henri, and Henri licked Bruce. They wagged their tails and tangled their leashes for a few seconds before Henri rolled on his back and played dead. Bruce copied.

"Henri's on good terms with the monkeys."

"Cool."

We watched them in silence for a moment, then Mimi said, "What's your favorite exhibit here?"

"The African painted dog. When people aren't getting stabbed in front of it."

"Totally. I marked it on my itinerary, but all that hoopla was a buzzkill. And when this guy came running toward us, Bruce got all jumpy."

"A free-the-animals type?"

"That, or he'd just witnessed somebody getting stabbed."

No bueno.

"What did he look like?" I asked. Mimi may have seen the perp and not realized it.

"Trailblazers jersey. Greg Oden. What a bust. Blue cargo shorts and some Air Force Ones." She rolled her eyes.

"You're all about that baller life," I said.

She shrugged. "Played in college. Then other pastures came calling."

Mimi was something.

My phone rang. Sims. I held up one finger and answered.

"PJ's coming," Sims said. "So no cheat meals till you hit the scale."

I started to tell him about Bentini, but he cut me off. He'd already heard.

"He'll heal," Sims said. "Don't talk to any cops. You hear me?"

I said "Si" and hung up.

"I love your old-man phone," Mimi said, nodding at my Jitterbug.

"I don't like all those fruits," I said.

We were making progress.

A part of me wanted more info on the hombre that had run from the crime scene, and another part of me wanted more time with Mimi. My track record with the female sex resembled the most tragic parabola of all time, but I wasn't deterred.

Misfortune breeds opportunity.

Two birds with one stone.

I gave her my best smile. "Wanna grab some coffee?"

4

We found seats at a café on a veranda overlooking the aviary, where the sun said hello every few minutes. Mimi had a small Frappuccino and I'd picked up a smoothie. Making weight tomorrow meant making sacrifices. Little to no solids before I hit the scale. Then all hell would break loose. Carbo-loading galore.

Mimi gazed out over the aviary. "I wonder how many warblers they have."

"About the same as turacos," I said. I pointed to the first bird I saw, and Mimi shook her head.

"That's a weaver."

"Where's the thread?"

Mimi laughed, and I took a sip of my smoothie. Banana-kale goodness.

"I was top badge in Girl Scouts," she said. "You have no aviary game."

I nodded. No comeback needed.

Then Henri nudged my knee and gave me his puppy eyes. He'd surpassed puppyhood months ago, but he wasn't a rookie when it came to begging. He knew the eyes did it every time. I pulled a napkin out of my pocket, unfolded it, and gave him two biscuits.

"You're quite the parent," Mimi said.

"Positive reinforcement yields positive canine qualities."

"Bruce hasn't left position," she said.

I looked down at Bruce. He stared me down like I was a frothy carnival barker.

"The biscuits are French," I said. I pulled out another one and held it near Bruce's nose. He gave me a nauseous look and turned his attention to the cash registers.

"Bruce lives for praise *sans* material possessions," Mimi said. She rubbed the top of Bruce's head, and he slobbered his appreciation.

I laughed, and we sat quietly for a couple minutes, taking in the birds and the vocals.

Then Mimi said, "Shame the warblers have to see this."

She pointed to the front of the cafe where two cops were buying coffee. They were either calling it quits after a long day or refueling to extend a long day. I didn't give a shit, so long as they stayed far away from our table. The cops were late to the Bentini party, and therein lay the problem. They needed to make a case, which meant they'd ruffle feathers and get bullshit statements. I'd been there—and I wasn't going back.

I slunk down in my chair.

"Some good that'll do," Mimi said. "A buff dude with a Doberman. Not the best camouflage."

"There're other service companions here."

"Right."

But the cops had only stopped in for coffee. A moment later, they were gone, and it was my turn to sleuth.

"How much did you see of the stabbing?" I asked.

"Less than I would have liked. Imagine paying twenty bucks to get stabbed in the stomach in broad daylight."

"Bad apples everywhere," I said.

"Respectable argument. But that guy had it coming. There's always a connection. I don't subscribe to the 'random attack at the zoo' theory."

I told Mimi about my connection to Bentini. I included the most pertinent parts and left out all the minutiae.

Mimi frowned. "I'm changing my tune on you."

"Madam, I doth protest."

"I knew those muscles weren't just for show."

"Indeed." I flexed my right bicep, and Mimi feigned delight.

She checked for the cops, then leaned in close.

"Your guy walked right into a pile of people. I was ten feet away with Bruce, tying my shoe. He had no social etiquette. Just about bumped a bunch of photogs."

"How many?" I said.

"Ten, twelve."

"How big were their bags?" I pictured a brazen one pulling out a knife and going to town.

"No bags. They wrapped the cameras around their necks. Those big DSLR ones with the fancy lenses."

"No bags? Wouldn't they try to keep them someplace safe? Those things cost mucho dinero."

Mimi shrugged. "I'm not the camera police. But yeah."

I took another sip of my smoothie. "Any identifying markers?"

"Is this how you charm the ladies?"

"Part pleasure and part business, missy. Unfinished business."

Mimi held my eyes for a second, then busted out laughing.

"You should do audiobooks if the boxing thing doesn't pan out. Sexy voice, Gedrin."

I smiled, but before I could add more wit, Mimi turned serious. "Not that I'm looking for that kinda thing. I'm super busy with work and stuff. Just came out here to enjoy the weekend with a friend."

"Bruce is great."

"No. My friend flaked on me."

"Male or female?"

"Why do you care?"

"It will impact my analysis."

Mimi rolled her eyes.

"Shame," I said. "Did he know it was a date, or was it supposed to be a friendly meetup?"

Mimi looked down and stubbed her shoe around. "No clue."

"Courtship is a very interesting experience," I said. "Can't quite predict the duration or the intensity. But you're in luck. I'm out of the game and don't wanna go back in right now. Just came out here to enjoy the weekend with a friend." I tilted my head at Henri.

One of the keys to attraction is to feign unattraction. Make them chase, hombre.

Mimi looked away. "Cool. Lot of cray-cray out there, that's for sure."

"Yep."

Mimi wasn't done.

"They say it gets easier with age. Like you're supposed to flip the switch and know how to make things work. One day you're this kid worrying about what kind of nail polish to wear to class, the next you're supposed to be Betty Crocker and hold it down. Do the whole nine-to-five and have dinner ready by seven. And get promoted and kick ass and get that ring and plan that ceremony. Pop out those little humans. Nobody tells you that while you're thinking about the rat race, your partner's screwing his therapist."

Awkward moments typically bring out the best in me. I have the perfect retort to save the day at all times. Once I lower my mandible my words soothe and heal and calm like chamomile. But this time I was flummoxed. I didn't want to be an asshole and gloss over her feelings, yet I didn't want to give a soliloquy. Not the time or the place.

I said, "Oxytocin is a strange bedfellow."

Mimi said nothing.

Then Bruce broke the silence, with three loud barks.

"He loves those damned balloons," Mimi said.

I looked back at the registers and saw a balloon maker fulfilling requests. Monkeys. Giraffes. Crabs. The maker had game, and Bruce had an eye for talent.

"If he can make one with Henri's face and Bruce's arms, I'll pay him triple," I said.

Mimi shook her head. "Bruce's front paws and Henri's back ones. That'll take the cake."

I finished the rest of my smoothie, and Mimi drank most of her caffeinated goodness before setting it aside. When Bruce barked again, I looked for the balloon maker, but he had disappeared.

Mimi pointed to the doors. "Basketball makes Bruce drool too."

"A regular Air Bud," I said.

"Still have unfinished business? You should look."

I turned to face the doors, and I saw what had gotten Bruce's attention. It was the man Mimi had described earlier—the one in the Blazers jersey, blue cargo shorts, and Air Force Ones.

5

reg Oden was touted as the next Shaq. Standing at seven-plus feet tall and tipping the scales at three hundred pounds, he commanded the paint and owned every rebound. He would have gone pro straight out of high school if it wasn't for the rule change. Instead, he played one year of college ball at Ohio State, where he led his team all the way to the championship game before bowing out to Florida. He was the consensus number one pick in that summer's NBA draft, even though the execs knew his dirty little secret: Oden had bum knees. Still, the Portland Trailblazers couldn't resist all the moolah from the season ticket holders. They drafted Oden number one overall, passing on a skinny kid named Kevin Durant. And the rest is history. Oden had more injuries than he did seasons in the league. Durant became a top player in the game for over a decade—and counting.

So I knew right then that the Blazers man loved Portland nostalgia. I'd use it all day to get the scoop. I'd ask all the right questions and he'd give all the right answers. At least, that's how it's supposed to work in the sleuth game. If things went awry, then it'd get real fun.

Bruce got to him first. He licked and sniffed, and then Henri joined the party. The Blazers man had blue cotton candy in one hand and a coffee cup in the other. He tensed up for a second, then relaxed.

"They're quite the rascals," Mimi said. She flashed her sexy smile, and the Blazers man was smitten just like I was.

"I have a pit," the Blazers man said. "Never could get him to see the sights. Not his sorta thing."

"We had to break legs to seal the deal in here," I said.

I held the man's gaze like he was one of my shitty opponents in the ring. I was testing him. While the average human avoided confrontation and went out of his way to avoid eye contact and stress and uncertainty, I embraced uncertainty. I relished it the way a thespian did the next casting call. While the average human sweated bullets, I was an ice sculpture.

We stood there, our eyes locked for an eternity. Just when I thought he was ready to break, the crows under his eyes perked up. I was close.

He blinked. To the victor go the spoils.

The Blazers man said, "You're freaking me out with those eyebrows, homie."

I nodded. "Swell."

The Blazers man looked me up and down like I had the plague. "Tall, fit, smug as hell. If it looks like a cop and talks like a cop, it's a fucking cop. I ain't sayin' shit."

Henri barked at a squirrel, and the man flinched.

"What kinda con are you?" I asked.

"Fuck you."

"Rehabilitation is the dirtiest word in town."

"I'm not going to no station, man. I know my rights."

"The African painted dog."

"What?"

"*Lycaon pictus*. Their home is in Africa. They run thirty miles an hour, hombre."

The Blazers man was confused as hell. That was all by design.

"But somebody got too knifey by the exhibit," I said, "and that's all she wrote. Gotta see the monkeys now."

Then it registered with Blazers man. He rubbed the crown of his head. "I ain't see shit."

"Say it again and I'll knock your ass all the way to your PO."

"Leave him out of this." The man stared me down some more and squinted for good measure. I could have put a stop to it in a heartbeat, but I preferred my interrogees to come to *moi* on their own.

"You box?" the man said.

"With the best of them."

He forced a smile.

"You're slower than Oden," I said.

"We shoulda won the chip already."

Mimi chimed in. "Not with Roy," she said.

She was right, but she was letting me run the show. Which was cool.

I told the Blazers man about my connection to Bentini. I added a few parts I hadn't mentioned to Mimi and took out a few parts that I'd emphasized with Mimi. The man rubbed the top of his scalp and looked both ways. Then he took a deep breath.

"I don't want any trouble with my PO," he said. "I didn't see shit."

"Remember what I said."

"I can't have any violations. My PO finds me ten inches from a crime scene, he files a violation and I go back in front

19

of my judge. He's gonna launch me, and I do a year bid easy."

"Min or max security?"

The Blazers man furrowed his brows. "Medium. Drug case."

"You have a public pretender?"

"Huh?"

"A public *defender*," Mimi said. "You know, the ones who slave away for hours on end with hundreds of cases and get no respect from judges, juries, prosecutors, or clients."

The Blazers man frowned. "I had one, and I got a good deal. But don't wanna chance it a second time in front of the judge."

"Say your piece and get the hell out of Dodge," I said. "Keep the zoo clean."

"I didn't see anything." The man shrugged. "One minute I'm at the painted dog, looking for that loco whatever to come out. Next minute, crowd scatters the hell away and the guy falls."

"How many people?"

"Ten, fifteen. Those bitch tourists who walk three wide with the cameras around their necks. You know what I'm saying?"

I nodded. "Any packs?" Backpacks. Fanny packs. Camera packs. Somewhere they could stash a knife.

"No. Just cameras. Shorts, t-shirts, sandals. Basic-ass tourists."

I rubbed my temples. Bentini didn't stab himself, and he didn't get stabbed by a camera either.

"When did you arrive on scene?" Mimi asked.

"I don't know. Can I go now?"

"Before or after the stabbing?" Mimi pressed. She looked

comfortable taking the lead and she asked questions far better than I did, so I rolled with it. Bruce held firm at her side.

"Like twenty seconds before. I'm there next to the crowd, and they scatter, man."

"Empty your pockets," Mimi said.

The Blazers man protested at first, but he must have realized that the quickest way to get us out of his hair was to comply, because he handed me his cotton candy stick and emptied his pockets, which consisted of a torn plume wallet, a state ID card, and three dollars in singles.

Three bucks. No wonder he qualified for a court-appointed lawyer.

"Happy?" he said.

I wasn't. "You didn't see shit, but what did you *hear?*" I said.

The Blazers man thought about it for a bit. I could see the gears churning in his head and could imagine the movie that was projecting on the inside of his skull. Just another day at the zoo, fun in the sun, then *bam*. What a shit show.

The Blazers man said, "When the crowd scattered, I heard your boy say 'Fink.'"

"Fink?"

"Yeah, Fink."

The Blazers man's phone rang. "Dammit. It's my PO." He finished his cotton candy and walked in the direction of the monkeys.

And I had a lead.

6

Mimi came back to my motel. For strictly platonic reasons. She felt for Bentini and wanted to solve the case just as much as I did. The Blazers man hadn't given me much, but hunches came in bunches. The perp had some connection to Bentini, judging by his excited utterance at the crime scene, and the perp also had some connection to me, judging by the note.

And of course Bentini had a connection to me. That was undoubtedly why he was at the zoo in the first place. Sims had sent him to spy on me, to make sure I was living life on the up-and-up prior to the Juko match. But as I thought that through, I knew there was no way Bentini touched down at Portland International and went straight to the monkeys. He would've caught a redeye last night and rested his head somewhere. And if you want to track your quarry, what better way to do so than by staying in the same place he is?

Keep your friends close and your enemies closer.

I was sure of it. Bentini had stayed at my motel.

I grabbed a mint as I walked up to the reception desk. A bubbly girl with plume hair greeted me.

"Do you have a reservation, sir?"

"I lost my key last night. This guy couldn't resist." I glanced down at Henri.

The girl typed into her computer. "Room number?"

I was in 206. The room across from me was 203. That would be the perfect hideout for a cutman's clandestine operation.

"203," I said.

More typing. I still couldn't operate a computer properly. I was unstoppable with the Jitterbug, but the screen was too small for comfort. I needed more pixels to hone all this wit. Maybe I'd annoy Sims about it till he caved and got me one for my birthday.

Six seconds later the girl said, "I'm reading that checkout was at eleven. I'm sorry, sir, but I need to charge a late fee. Company policy."

"The motels in Idaho would quake in their boots with byzantine procedures like that." I had no idea if that was the case, but my mind was a dictionary sometimes and it sounded right. Truth be told, Sims had always wanted me to stay in five-star places for security reasons, but a shoebox surrounded by bars changes your perspective. I was team shitty motel any day of the week. Late checkout included.

The girl frowned. "This isn't Idaho, I'm afraid. I just need some ID, sir, and I'll give you a duplicate key, on the house. I'll add the late checkout to your final invoice."

I couldn't comply. One look at my ID and the jig was up. The girl would call the cops and I'd enter Oregon's criminal lack-of-justice system while Juko talked shit to HBO about me dodging the fight. But then again, it ain't over till it's over. Fake it till you make it. The girl might wither under my fine features and give me a pass, or recognize that I busted skulls for a living and ask for an autograph. Or any combo in between.

"I'll only be a minute," I said. "Left my camera bag up there."

The bubbly girl wasn't buying it, but Mimi stepped in.

She gave me a sympathetic smile, then spoke to the girl in a hushed tone. "Ever since the accident, he's been quite forgetful. Doctor says it'll take another year for his vertebrae to fuse right and his mind to follow. And with all those meds, you know how it goes. Down there. When he proposed, I never could have imagined this life." She looked tearful as she spoke. Oscar material.

The bubbly girl was no longer so bubbly. She was speechless.

Then she punched something into her computer and handed Mimi a keycard. "Please be quick. Housekeeping has to get to it before the zoo crowd shows."

Mimi thanked her and patted me on the head like I was a small child, and we walked to the elevator.

"You come in handy," I said.

"I'm quite the prop, huh?"

"Spoken like a true thespian. You didn't even use Bruce."

"That'd be cheating."

"I'll say."

We took the elevator up to the second floor, which was also the top floor. Still, the very fact it had an elevator gave it three stars. The green concrete walkway that lined the floor bumped it back down to two, and then the three soda machines got it back up to three.

As we walked, the floor morphed into a Morocco red. The contractors must have run out of green paint. I stopped at 206 and opened it up.

"I don't think this is a good idea," Mimi said.

"They either learn to be social without their parents or they lose all privileges," I said.

Mimi nodded, and we ushered Bruce and Henri inside. Then I shut the door and crossed over to 203.

"This is gonna make for a great story someday," Mimi said.

"The nuptials of the century."

Room 203 looked like any other room in any other motel in any other part of the land. The TV was on, and a suitcase lay open on the bed. An ironing board was set up by the window.

I searched the place. Drawers, cabinets. Under the bed and the box spring. All seven compartments of Bentini's suitcase.

Nada.

"Check the balcony while you're making the place look pretty," Mimi said.

I gestured for her to take the lead. "Ladies first."

Mimi smiled and checked the balcony.

Nada again.

I searched the drawers again, and I found it. In the night-stand drawer right by the bed. Peeking out of the Yellow Pages and joined to a money clip.

A receipt.

A receipt that didn't make sense.

Bentini had a driving lesson tomorrow at ten a.m. in Pahrump, Nevada, at Spring Mountain Motor Resort. Every auto aficionado's wet dream. Speed and muscle and steel and rubber. It'd be one hell of a lesson, that's for sure.

But it'd take over an hour to get back to Vegas for my weigh-in. Bentini either planned for the shortest lesson in the history of lessons, or he planned to ditch my big day.

Something was up. And so was my search, because a voice spoke up behind me.

"Stop touching material evidence, or you're going back to the pen."

7

wo Columbo wannabes were standing in the doorway. One wore gray khakis, a light purple button-down tucked in, and black tennis shoes. The other wore a navy suit with black penny loafers. I pegged the penny loafers hombre as the rookie, and the khaki hombre as the jefe.

Three seconds later I was right.

Khaki Man walked in first. "Can you explain why you're walking all over my crime scene when the vic's still in the hospital and he never authorized any sort of property retrieval?"

Penny Loafer Man smirked.

I was puzzled. I looked both men up and down for a minute straight, my eyes hard, my body still as a statue. Sal had taught me all the tricks of the fight game. Stare your opponent into submission. Until they break. Everybody breaks. To the victor go the spoils.

I kept staring, and even when Khaki Man tried to break the

silence, I shushed him like a momma does her munchkins on the playground. He bit his tongue and crinkled his nose. Then, when I was confident I had a fully captive audience, I exercised my mandible.

"I don't have to explain shit," I said. "My friend got his ass stabbed at the zoo and y'all left the crime scene to play Hieronymus Bosch. They teach ineptitude at the academy, or that the first time you pissed yourselves when you had to throw down?"

Khaki Man cracked his knuckles. "Wise guy, hand over whatever that is in your hand. You're obstructing an attempted murder investigation."

I took one last look at the receipt. I'd already committed the important details to my cabeza, but I wasn't going to let him get off that easy. I rolled it up into a basketball and shot it at Penny Loafers. He came prepared though, and during my little soliloquy had put gloves on. He caught the receipt, unwrinkled it, took out a magnifying glass, and pretended to analyze the thing right then and there.

Khaki Man shook his head. "This isn't the movies. You're one step away from eating bologna sandwiches for the weekend."

I shrugged. "Easy-peasy. These chompers have eaten four thousand over the last twelve years." I'd overstated my bologna intake on the inside, but it had the desired effect.

Khaki Man clenched his right fist and would have thrown a tragic punch if Penny Loafers hadn't intervened at that moment by handing over the receipt. Khaki Man put it into an evidence bag.

Then Penny Loafers found his courage.

"Multiple wits put you at the scene kneeling next to the vic. Saying things to the vic. Holding the vic's hand."

"Blimey," I said.

"Hard to miss the biggest dude in the room with two brain cells left," Khaki Man said.

It was amateur hour. Every lawman knew the good-cop, bad-cop routine. Play off the weakness of the subject till he or she confesses. Offer a soda, a sandwich, or absolution from the man upstairs. If that doesn't work, offer a deal you have no authority to make. Anything to get the job done. And if that doesn't work, then the bad cop threatens the world till the subject caves. I wasn't surprised by the routine, but I was surprised that both of the badges were playing bad cop. Maybe the hombres missed interrogation day at the academy.

Penny Loafers kept on the bad routine. "You were saying something, real close. Like y'all had a secret. Maybe y'all were in on it to get insurance money. That's usually how it goes. Stage the crime scene and let the poor civil servants figure it out. I hate secrets, man. They raise my cholesterol and wifey says we need family therapy." He smirked, and Khaki Man joined in.

I said, "Since this is a half-assed interrogation, I'd be remiss if I didn't ask a few questions myself."

"We're not answering your—"

"Who in the blue hell are you? A mall cop, PI, fed, statie? I don't give a flying fuck, but at the very least I should get your name and badge number before I lawyer up. You know how it goes."

Penny Loafers went silent.

Khaki Man said, "I could take you downtown right now for assaulting a PO."

I said, "Respect is a two-way street. A name for a name."

"We already *know* your name," Khaki Man said. "Half the world does with your antics in Chicago. We don't play those games out here, son. But I suppose the rubber must meet the road sometime. And I know you'll fuck up sooner or later. Best we get acquainted, Gedrin." He held out his hand. "Detective Ben Finley. Portland Police Bureau." He flashed his badge and smiled. His pearly whites hadn't seen a brush for quite some time. They were like traffic cones.

No bueno.

I thought about giving him a left hook, but I'd be able to feel Sims's heart attack across state lines. So I shook Finley's hand like a gentleman.

Then I looked over at Penny Loafers. "And you, señor?"

He stared daggers, then followed the lead of the man in charge. "Detective Yaz Edgar. You know the rest." He opened his suit jacket and showed me his badge.

"Fancy schmancy," I said.

"Where are your manners?" Finley snapped.

"No comprendo."

He tilted his head toward Mimi. "You gonna push your woman all the way into the corner or you gonna introduce us proper?"

I'd forgotten all about Mimi during my party with Portland's finest. I was allergic to the blue, and tunnel vision followed whenever I engaged them. But Mimi was good. She'd let me ride or die solo as I traded barbs with the detectives.

Now she stepped forward.

"Assistant Public Defender Tanya Mimi. I work downtown at the courthouse, Detective, and let's just say this little fiesta was highly entertaining, but completely unproductive. Somebody stabbed that man, and this investigation is becoming a shit show. Keep grasping at straws and I'll make sure to call your sergeant first thing Monday morning."

Finley said nothing.

Edgar said nothing.

And I said nothing.

Damn, indigent defense lawyers have game. I rethought my stance on the matter right then and there.

Mimi walked out the door, and I followed. But as I walked past the two detectives, Finley had to get the last word.

"Yo, Gedrin," he said. "My money's on Juko kicking your ass without breaking a sweat."

8

Mimi gave me a ride to the hospital, but we detoured for flowers. She wanted orchids, and I wanted a candy bar, but I still couldn't have solids. We found a shop two blocks away from St. Vincent's Hospital with a big ole titanium door and a wooden sign out front from Prohibition. I waited in the car while Mimi picked the perfect hues for Bentini. I told her he didn't want any pizzazz, but she insisted. Then I shut my mandible. I learned early on in life never to question a woman's floral game. Deflect, ignore, nod your head at all the right times. Speak only when spoken to and you'll make it out alive. Life is about vibes. Scary ones and hangry ones and chill ones. My thoughts skewed toward the latter. Mimi was a wildcard. A part of me wondered if she lived life on the edge or full of regrets. That said a lot about a woman. Even though she was a platonic companion, my brain couldn't stop connecting the dots. It started with the cotton candy.

Ninety seconds later Mimi came back with a gargantuan

bouquet and a box of chocolates. She tossed the box like a frisbee.

"For you, sweetie."

I said, "I have to make weight."

"They'll keep, then. They were on sale, but they're still good for a while." She smiled and backed her green Honda Civic out of the parking lot. When she turned onto Monterey, one of Bruce's fur balls floated in the air and lodged itself on the rearview mirror. Mimi sped up, and for a second I wondered if she missed Indy.

"You gotta use the furminator," I said.

"Even when the monster's not here, he's here. Gizmos be damned."

Henri and Bruce were probably in their twelfth game of hide-and-seek now. Either that or they were both mush. Henri lost interest easily, but with Bruce all bets were off.

Mimi found the hospital and parked in the visitor's garage. I reached for my wallet, but Mimi told me you get a ticket and pay for it at the end.

"Besides," she said, "I brought you here, so I'm paying. End of story."

"Spoken like a true counselor," I said.

She laughed, and I realized this was the first time a lawyer had ever ponied up their dinero for me. Usually fees rolled off a lawyer's tongue the way features rolled off a used car sales-man's. They ran their mouths till they got the last breath and they left you in the dust. In all my years, I've made friends with humans of all shapes, sizes, ethnicities, religions, and occupations. They liked my wit and grit and fashion sense. But I had far too few amigos in the lawyer column. Maybe it was philosophical differences or maybe it was Chicago or maybe it was the way they smiled. But Mimi was different. She was the real deal. She fought every day for the underdog and then got shat on by judges, prosecutors, clients, and the general public. But she didn't back down and had the balls to keep going. For the love of the game. She wore the public defender mantle with pride as she went to war with the Finleys of the world.

Mimi was growing on me.

We walked right up to reception and asked for Bentini's room. I brought my chocolates, planning to re-gift them to my cutman. Once the applesauce left his system, he couldn't say no to cocoa. We found an elevator and took it up to the fifth floor. We got out, hung a left, then two rights, and found the room. Bentini didn't have the connects, because a curtain separated the room and he shared his misery with a decrepit lady a few feet away. She was asleep. Mimi and I tiptoed past her, pulled the curtain back, and found Bentini watching TV.

"Ah, my favorite employer," Bentini said.

I gave him the box of chocolates and Mimi gave him the flowers. She frowned for a second, then was all smiles.

"You'd think I was on death's door," Bentini said.

"A couple more inches and adios amigo," I said.

"Nah. It looked far worse than what it really was." Bentini raised his bed with that magic button on the side, then pressed another button.

For the meds.

"Easy does it," Mimi said. "Don't get too greedy."

"So I've been told. I'm a stubborn mule. This one knows better than anybody. When did you two start dating?" He looked at Mimi, then at me, then at Mimi again.

Mimi blushed. "No, it's not like that."

I smiled. "We're two very civil strangers who happened upon an unfortunate event."

Bentini shook his head. "Sims wanted you on a tight leash. Always the man in control. The fixer. But he couldn't stop this, could he?" He lifted his gown and showed me the wound by his ribs. I'd seen worse, but this was damned close to worse.

"Who was it?" I asked.

"Let it be," Bentini said.

"I'm gonna find that asshole and get to the bottom of it."

"Spoken like a petulant child. You've got to fight, Gedrin. Get that through your stupid head. You didn't come back from the dead to throw it all away. Sal's gonna have a heart attack if he hears this shit."

If Sal saw the box of chocolates he'd have a heart attack, but Bentini was right. I'd agreed to the fight for a reason. I looked out the window at the parking garage. Hundreds of cars standing pat while their owners experienced all stages of the human condition. Birth. Death. Renewal from the brink of death. Life was the ultimate novel, filled with the ultimate cliffhangers. Some would say choosing to bash somebody's brains in for a living fast-tracked my novel's ending. Some would say destiny works in mysterious ways. No matter how it all played out, I firmly believed it was better to live fifty kick-ass years than a hundred boring ones.

"What fight?" Mimi asked.

Bentini gave me a puzzled look.

Even lawyers missed the eight ball sometimes.

Then Mimi grinned. "Psych. ESPN is a litigator's best pill sometimes."

Bentini laughed. "She's a keeper."

We stood there for a minute soaking it all in.

Then Bentini said, "I'm getting discharged in a few hours. Meds will have my levels all over the damned place, but I'll be at weigh-in."

I said, "Save it for another day. Don't kill yourself."

"I haven't been in the ring all these years and now you

wanna replace me for this pretty lady?" He winked at Mimi and furrowed his brows at me.

"Your pops would be proud," I said.

Bentini grew serious. "How's that?"

"You making an impact in the fight game. You almost get stabbed to death and you're back out there like it's a warmup, bro. You're one tough sonofabitch."

Bentini looked out the window for a few seconds. I couldn't tell if he was going to berate me for bringing up his old man, or if he was going comic again.

Mimi must have sensed the awkwardness because she excused herself from the room.

Bentini looked me up and down like I had the plague, and then he said, "This isn't an easy fight, Gedrin. This one's gonna be your hardest yet. Forget about me. Keep your head in the game."

"I'm always in the game."

"I hope so."

And that's when I sprung it on him. "What's with the damned motor track?"

I hadn't forgotten the receipt. Finley had it now, but I had the man himself. And the eyes tell the long and short of it, no matter the bullshit that comes out of the mouth.

The eyes don't lie.

I stared Bentini down for an eternity, and then he grinned.

"Leadership training," he said.

Before I could ask more, three white gowns threw back the curtain and started checking his vitals. They had clipboards and computers and attitudes. They kicked me out, and as I left the ancient lady smiled at me with no teeth.

9

Three hours later I was on a private jet with Mimi, Henri, Bruce, two stewardesses, and one pilot. When Sims offered the PJ, how could I refuse? Point A to B in record time, style, and comfort. I could stretch my legs and sing whatever tunes I wanted sans interruption. Sometimes it took a minute to find the right tune, but once I found it, I was all in. If the tune had rhythmic musicality, I dubbed it a success. If not, I ditched it faster than a moldy pair of socks.

I closed my eyes and browsed the mental menu, going through all the genres.

Nada.

I crinkled my nose like Finley and shook my head. Fight weekend did that to me. Fucked with my nerves of steel and made my middle name insomnia. My stomach twisted, my chest fluttered, and my neck muscles tightened like an anaconda. The haters called me a geriatric in a Greek god's body. And every body had an expiration date. Some came sooner than others and at the most inopportune times. Too many miles and down goes Frazier. I'd melt like butter and that'd be all she wrote. The sharks would have a field day, but I wasn't doing them any favors. They'd have to carry me out in a body bag before I quit the game.

I propped a neck pillow on my headrest and stretched out. I closed my eyes again, and just when I was about to get some sleep, I felt drool on my cheeks.

I sprang up. Henri was slobbering all over the furniture. He'd gone easy on my section, but he'd used his teeth on all the others. He didn't apologize for his actions, and I didn't scold him. High altitudes mess with the canine brain. I was sure of it. Plus, if you don't fully catch your furry friend in the act, the corrective effect equals zero. The literature don't lie. I took a note to catch the rascal next time.

As I sat down again, Henri came back around and tried to slobber on my fine features, but I wasn't gonna let him touch this moneymaker again. Right when he opened his mouth I tossed him a tennis ball the size of two steaks. Henri grunted and took off like a rocket.

"Nervous?" Mimi said.

She was in the seat diagonal to me. She flashed her pearly whites and flipped her hair to one side. We were still in platonic territory, and I guess that covered private jets and fights and amateur sleuthing. Two's always better company, so I'd asked her to join me for the weekend. Fun times lay ahead. She'd see me kick Juko's ass and she'd be smitten with all my testosterone. Or she'd see Juko kick my ass, and she'd comfort me in defeat and probably still be smitten. Win-win. Not that I was keeping score. But damn it felt good to have a beautiful woman in my orbit again. Murphy's law was still a thing, but you gotta take the crookeds with the straights.

I stuck my tongue out. "I was built for this game."

"Spoken like a true neurotic."

"Gracias."

Mimi rubbed Bruce's head, and he whined like a puppy. Henri looked at me, then at the tennis ball, then at Bruce. The ultimate test. Permission to play or not to play, master? I caved, and Henri kicked the tennis ball to Bruce with his paws. They played.

"They're really into it," Mimi said. She watched the canine Olympics, and the stewardesses took out their phones and snapped pictures.

"Those are some fine stewardesses," I said.

"Disgusting," Mimi said.

"They're the quintessential professionals. How many would let them roll around the floor with a jumbo tennis ball at thirty thousand feet, no questions asked?"

"The rules don't apply to celebs."

"I'm a D-lister on a good day."

"No such thing, champ. Everybody's got game with social media."

"I love my Jitterbug."

"Wow."

Mimi fished in her purse and pulled out a black leather case. No more than six by eight. She opened the front flap and it lit up faster than a Christmas tree. She stared at it for a little bit, then tapped right. And right. And right. She did it ten times. Then stopped.

"Online chess is horrible," I said.

"It's a Kindle," Mimi said.

"What?"

Mimi told me all about it, and I crossed another technological marvel off my ignorance list. I was a dinosaur a few weeks ago, but now I was a lion. Pride and progress. Evolving in this new land. But old habits die hard. I could see the efficiency of the Kindle. A million books in the palm of your hand. But I couldn't believe the sacrifice. The musty smell of a good ole fashioned paperback was muy bueno. I'd take Grisham and Clancy and Marlowe and Parker by hand any day of the week.

Mimi went back to reading, and we fell silent for a few minutes.

Then I spoke. "You don't have to follow me. Have fun while you're out here. Don't feel beholden." I didn't want her to think the trip came with any strings attached. I enjoyed her company and that was that. Of course, I couldn't control her brain, but at least I'd cleared mine.

She looked up from her book. "Don't sweat it. I like tagging along. Most fun I've had in weeks. The courtroom can get pretty stuffy."

"'Tis the world's grandest stage."

"When you're in the trenches every day the first thing you want is to get the hell out of there and forget all that shit."

"You make a compelling argument, counselor. Those hombres on *Law & Order* are depressed as hell. Every episode."

Mimi rolled her eyes.

"You should learn to box," I said.

"Why?"

"Best cardio of all time. Blow some steam. And you never know when it'll come in handy."

"Are you saying I'm fat?"

I froze. Do not engage.

"Not quite."

She softened. "I guess you have a point. Should start somewhere. Knock those creepos out sniffing around the park. Can't get a good run in for the life of me."

"Learn to throw that jab, and you'll be chillin' like a villain."

"Your trainer cool with you spilling all these secrets? I'm distracting you too much."

"So long as I don't eat any pancakes, we're straight."

Mimi smiled. "Thanks."

"De nada."

"Are you Spanish? Those words roll off your tongue a lot, and you have a great accent."

"No."

"Okay." She left it, and I didn't elaborate. There was always a method to one's madness and a magician never revealed his secrets. I was a Spaniard at heart, and I'd leave it at that. A little mystery went a long way.

A few minutes later, the pilot's voice came over the speakers. He was preparing us for landing in Pahrump. Henri and Bruce were on top of their game. They ditched the tennis ball, lay down next to each other, and waited it out.

Mimi looked at me. "Pahrump is not exactly Vegas."

I smiled. "I've got a need for speed."

We landed. Henri and Bruce went into an Escalade and Mimi and I found an Uber. I tipped the Escalade driver extra and told him to take the canines straight to Sims. He had plenty of space, and by the time he realized what was up I'd be making progress.

The driver tore off, and we did too.

I didn't make any conversation with the Uber man, but Mimi sure did. The driver laughed at all the right times and blushed at all the others. Ten minutes later we reached our destination. I might have had a big fight coming up, but I still had unfinished business. I don't forgive and I don't forget. Mess with my seconds and you pay the price. Family is family. I'd follow every lead and ask every question till I got answers.

When we pulled up to the racetrack though, somebody had thrown a wrench in my plans.

A chain-link fence surrounded the parking lot, and a big sign in the middle read "No Trespassing. Violators will be prosecuted."

10

"The bumper cars went out of style," Mimi said.

I didn't understand. Why would Bentini have a lesson at a shuttered facility? He saved every penny like it was his last. He wasn't a rocket scientist, but he wasn't green either.

Mimi was studying the no-trespassing sign. "Looks new," she said. She pointed to the paint. I wasn't a paint connoisseur by any means, but I saw it too. No rust. No jagged corners. No faded letters. The paint was so fresh it made your nose hairs tickle. An olfactory explosion of chemicals.

"If he knew the place was closed he wouldn't book," I said. "They took his booking, ergo the place was open at the time of booking."

"Great work, Sherlock." Mimi smiled and stuck out her tongue. She walked along the fence, and I told the Uber driver he could take off. Or at least that's what I wanted to do. When I turned, he was already gone. So much for customer service in the Sagebrush State. Hell, I'd had better in the Big Apple.

Mimi came back a few seconds later. "Not a crack in the armor."

"A lawyer thinking of violating the law? I knew y'all were shysters."

"We analyze statutes and think of avenues to exploit them. Within the lines, of course."

"To the cheater go the spoils," I said.

"Whatever."

The fence blocked the way in, but I could still see the place. A brownstone clubhouse, a swimming pool, and a hotel sat smack dab in the center of six miles of track built for adrenaline junkies. Shutting down the whole enchilada had to be expensive. I wondered how much money the place was losing per day. I was trying to run the numbers in my head, when I was interrupted.

"We've been out of commission for a while."

I turned and found a linebacker standing a few feet away. I couldn't tell if he played pro or not, but he sure as hell played some ball somewhere back in the day. The man's neck muscles looked like they were glued to the bottom of his ears, and his quads were two big-ass tree trunks. His biceps were twenty inches easy, and his triceps were a perfect horseshoe shape.

I was a tad jealous.

"The website doesn't agree," I said.

"I don't run the damned website," the man said.

"Who does?"

"Have no idea."

"What's your esteemed position here?"

"Security."

"At a closed venue?"

The man furrowed his brows. "Since the lawsuit, we've needed more eyes on the place. So they send in Vic Parson.

There's twenty security guards on payroll, but it's always gotta be Vic Parson. The assholes."

I wanted to ask if he was Parson, but I also wanted my face intact for the fight. If Parson threw a sucker punch, hell, it'd be a long day for Sims.

Mimi said, "Your services are much appreciated. Those slip and falls can be super costly."

Parson shook his head. "Ain't no fall. Some young 'un got too cute on the track, and there you have it. Family had some of them real fancy lawyers. Wrongful death lawsuit. And here we are. Guarding the fences. For miles." Parson pulled out a cigarette and took a drag.

"When did you close?" I said.

"Three weeks ago."

"My friend booked a driving lesson for tomorrow."

"Take it up with them nerds running the computers. Maybe he'll get a refund. But the way they run this place, I would manage expectations."

"Who runs the track?" I said.

Parson offered me a cigarette, and I declined. Periodic asthma with periodic nicotine was no bueno. He offered one to Mimi and she declined too.

"You reporters be asking too many questions," he said.

I was proud. My amateur sleuthing had given me a journalistic vibe. Barbara Walters, step aside.

"What kinda reporter doesn't have a notepad?" I said.

Parson shook his head. "Technology is funny sometimes. Don't need pen and paper these days. I seen microphones smaller than your pinky, man. Chips in your ear. Shit taped to your ass."

"The chips must be painful," I said.

"Move along," Parson said. "My break's almost over."

"Isn't it a perpetual break if nobody's watching?"

Parson grunted. "They're always watching."

I was one step closer to Parson having had enough. And having enough meant he'd take things into his own hands. That'd be the physical manifestation. But then there's the mental manifestation. Parson would let something slip. Right out his mandible before his brain even realized what the hell he was doing.

I waited for it.

Parson tossed his cigarette into the grass and stubbed it out with his toe. "If you're not a reporter, I suppose there ain't no harm in extending this conversation. For socialization purposes. Gets quiet round here when the heat says hello."

Bingo. Rapport is rapport.

"Full disclosure," I said. "She's a lawyer." I pointed to Mimi, and she raised her hands up as if to say 'what the hell.'

"From a long line of lawyers," she said.

I said, "You can't trust a long line."

Mimi's face turned red.

Parson eyed me like I had the plague. "Boy, you've got jokes, but one day those jokes are gonna come back to bite you in the ass."

"Tell me something new. Who runs Track C?" Bentini's receipt was seared in my mind. The place was so damned big there were multiple tracks. He'd had a lesson on Track C. Common sense dictated that if there was a Track C, there was also a Track A and B, unless the owners labeled things for feng shui. Hell, in that case Track Z could be around the corner.

Parson narrowed his eyes. "There's where the accident happened. One of the worst I've seen, and I've been here twenty years this December."

"Bad instructor?" I said.

"They're bogus. Taking people for a ride tryin' to teach 'em to drive fast. None of them assholes were pros. What they gonna teach? Those that can't do, teach. My fifth grade teacher sang it to the heavens and bless her soul she was right. They gonna have more blood on their hands here."

"Did you raise these concerns to management?" Mimi asked. She was no doubt thinking of some legal angle to all this and I wasn't, but lawyers had a method to their madness. I was asking questions that she might already have the answers to.

Parson laughed. "Nobody gives a shit what the black man in the security booth says. So long as that green be coming in, back up that Brink's truck. Now they gonna need it with that lawyer."

Mimi smiled.

"What's the instructor's name?" I asked.

Parson said, "Now we're about crossing that line. You ever teach this man here about confidentiality?" He looked to Mimi for support.

She shook her head. "Confidentiality applies from the corporation to the lawyer. Management holds the privilege, but it doesn't trickle down to independent contractors."

I took Mimi's word for it.

"How you know I'm independent?" Parson asked.

Mimi smiled. "A long line of lawyers. And the name on the back of your jacket. 'Rosco's Security.'"

Mimi 1, Parson 0.

I said, "You're off the hook, hombre."

Parson stretched his shoulder blades back, and for a moment I thought he'd elbow Mimi and sucker punch me. I wouldn't complain. Bring on the surprises. I relished them the way society relished all those damned fruit phones. Then he looked across the parking lot, past the ramps and the tracks and the pool in back, and his eyes settled on something a hundred yards out, but I couldn't see it.

"I used to come here as kid," he said. "With my pops. One

45

track back in those days. And nobody complained. No lines and fights and fancy Latin legal papers. Everybody appreciated that sunlight. Now, forget it." He looked me in the eye. "The asshole who did this works a second gig on Flamingo Road. If you see him tell him he should do time for the kid."

I said, "No prob."

11

M imi called an Uber, and a few minutes later the driver with no customer service showed up again. He had a Slurpee in one hand and a cigar in the other. He apologized for hightailing it out of Dodge and begged for a five-star review. He claimed he was still on the patch and adjusting to the new order of things *sans* nicotine.

"Step on it," I said.

I gave him the address, and we left Parson in the dust. I knew one place on Flamingo Road that fit the bill. Parson didn't give me the particulars, and I didn't ask for them. It didn't take a scholar to know the spot where all the aspiring entrepreneurs went to play.

Spring Valley had over two hundred thousand suburbanites plying their craft just two miles from the Strip. The homey feel made it one of the chiller places to live in Clark County. Sims had wanted to move my camp there several times, but when Sal and I united on an issue it was adios, amigo. Routine ran the fight game.

The driver picked up speed on the 215 and passed two

white vans headed to summer camp. The cool kids in back flicked us off and spat on the glass. Nobody chided the kids, so they flicked us off again and spat on the glass with more intensity this time. They were the players and we were in the mezzanine, soaking in the show. I wondered if they were on the way to football camp, astrology camp, or fat camp. Those were the big three during my title run. My bet was on fat camp, but I was biased. I went to fat camp. Not as a participant, but as a trainer. Best summer gig I ever had.

I looked over at Mimi to tell her all about it, but she was knocked out. From an attempted murder to coffee with a stranger to asshole detectives to a PJ, I couldn't blame her. The Gedrin lifestyle had so many plot twists it'd make Agatha Christie proud.

Seven minutes later Mimi woke up and said, "We're not in Kansas anymore."

"You missed three bales of hay a mile back," I said.

Mimi rubbed her eyes and cracked her neck twice. "Damn. That's a first."

"The trapezius muscles are prone to perpetual tightness. The struggle is real."

"No, I normally can't sleep for shit."

That made two of us. The last time I got sound sleep was when the Bulls won their sixth title. Like my love life, my sleeping patterns mirrored an insane parabola.

Mimi looked at me. "You like doing this stuff," she said. It was a statement, not a question.

"Si."

Mimi looked out her window and enjoyed the mountaintops that peeked out from the beltway. She said nothing for a few minutes, then the driver said something that I forgot, then I told Mimi my plan.

"That's not sound at all," she said.

"Keep knocking on doors and one's gonna open up. Simple mathematics."

"Yeah. It'll open, all right. Right into some psycho's hands with a shotgun and a trench coat at the stroke of midnight. Waiting for you with bated breath."

"What makes breath bated?" I said.

"You're ridiculous," Mimi said.

"Slasher films are no bueno," I said.

She punched me in the shoulder. We were making progress. I still wasn't keeping score, but physical touch is the first step to intimacy. Even a rookie knew that.

The driver crossed a bridge and took exit 21 onto Flamingo Road, and a minute later we reached our destination. I told the driver to ditch the patch for good and to fucking wait this time. Mimi overruled me and told him to never come back.

So much for five stars.

We went in.

The place looked like a shiny new duffel bag. The mirrors glistened and the floors smelled like lilacs. Sal would give the place two thumbs way down, and then he'd give the owner a hard right hand to the kisser.

Sal and him had a longstanding beef.

Me too.

Hava Nowa's Boxing Gym prided itself on upscale clientele and an upscale training experience. Hava Nowa himself trained some of the world's best fighters. He trained them for free, soaking in all the publicity and adding zeros to his bank account. But the true asshole came out with the average Joes. He charged them five ransoms to run the treadmill and work the heavy bag around the pros. Average meant suits like Mimi, but taking advantage was taking advantage.

But that wasn't why I had a beef with Nowa.

He was my second.

Back in the day.

Nowa and Sal and Bentini.

Together they were the three musketeers defending their prized possession: me. We flew up the ranks, decimating opponents and changing boxing forever. The dream team. The Beatles. The papers had a new name after every fight. Bentini fixed my face and Sal talked shit in the corner and Nowa worked the cameras. But eventually egos collide and someone feels like the odd man out. Nowa got greedy. He wanted to be head trainer and he wanted more pay and a take of Sal's gym proceeds. That, and he wanted to change Sal's game plan every time. But my allegiance was always to Sal, and that only accelerated the hombre's shrewdness. Nowa ditched me mid-camp right before I picked up my case. And as a final fuck you, he took the rest of Sal's pro fighters and set up shop in Spring Valley right on good ole Flamingo Road.

I wanted a piece of him.

"Why's that one bag so tiny?" Mimi asked. She pointed to the speed bag and I told her all about it as we walked over to an empty station.

"Hold your hands like pythons and keep going at it," I said. I showed her how, and she was a natural.

"Don't we have to pay first?" Mimi said.

This was all part of my plan. Enter a fancy gym and the untrained mind starts thinking green. How much and when and how. But the sly mind thinks of schooling the system. Pissing off the higher-ups to get a reaction. I gave it three minutes for Nowa to come out.

Then the fun would begin.

"Don't worry about it," I said. "Let me see those hands."

Mimi went to work, and I smiled. I wasn't up to Sal's caliber by any means, but I could motivate when the time was right. Mimi had a tool in her arsenal now that she didn't have five minutes ago with the Slurpee driver.

Progress.

A minute later, Mimi stopped.

"No cheating," I said. "Chop chop."

Mimi shook her head. "That guy's freaking me out." She was looking past the speed bags and the heavy bags and the treadmills and the medicine balls to the middle of the ring. I followed her gaze till I found him.

Juko.

Staring right at us.

"He's two fries short of a happy meal," I said. "Forget him."

Juko smirked at me, walked to his corner, and whispered to a man with his back to us.

"Here comes the cavalry," Mimi said.

"Can't wait."

Hava Nowa turned around, put his hand on Juko's shoulder as if to say great work, and then he walked around the ring and over to us. While the last twelve-plus years had been kind to Sal, I couldn't say the same for the Flamingo man. He had red facial hair, mutton chops, and a belly that looked like five inflatable floaties. And his teeth were atrocious. They looked like he hadn't seen the dentist in two years easy.

"Juko take all your Crest?" I asked.

Nowa scowled. "Shame on you, Gedrin. You know the rules. Can't mess with a fighter's camp till the weigh-in."

I smiled. As a matter of professional courtesy. I'd be ready for the weigh-in.

"Your boy pissed himself the minute he saw me," I said.

"Two days," Nowa said. "The world will see the real champ. Not some prison has-been. Next year this time he'll be walking with that title around his waist. But forgive me. How's Sal? Haven't had lunch with the old man in a while."

I wanted to give him an uppercut right there, but that would have been too easy.

"He says a lightweight's a lightweight," I said. "But fair play. My name works wonders out west." I glanced around the gym and raised my eyebrows in an uninspired way.

Nowa gritted his teeth. "You never listened. That's always been your problem. Your way or the highway. You have a corner for a reason, son." He eyed Mimi suggestively. "How do you put up with him?"

Mimi laughed. "I train hard."

"The right attitude." He smiled at Mimi, but she didn't return it.

"I'm down a cutman," I said.

If Nowa was surprised, he didn't show it. "News travels fast round here. Sucks for Maximo. Hope him a speedy recovery."

"Speedy like a racetrack."

I trained my eyes on Nowa like he was about to get it. I kept them there, waiting for him to flinch and roll over. But he was good.

Nada.

"You were never satisfied with the green," I said. "Always wanted more stacks and more fun. Taking side gigs to pad the gross. Pathetic. You killed a kid, man."

Nowa was unfazed. "I've been racing since I was nine. Like you would know. Threw away your prime and now you're playing fucking detective round here. Jealous of what I've built, that's all."

"The track's closed and your lesson with Bentini is buried. Or it would have been, if not for Detective Finley. He's a real jealous sonofabitch."

Nowa looked around his gym and marveled at all the people putting in work. He hadn't heard what I had to say, or at least that was the front that he put up. I knew he'd heard every damned word. When the truth hits you smack dab in the face, you run or you hide.

Nowa was running.

"Your boy was a fuckup through and through," Nowa said. "When you went in, he went down and was always looking for a quick buck. Without his pops to give him an allowance, what good was he? Smart in the head, but stupid in the real world. He worked a couple corners with me, then he hit the bottle too much and I kicked his ass out. I can't have that riffraff around my gym. Last I heard, when he sobered back up he wanted to drive."

"Learned from the best," I said.

"No. The open road. Transport. Big rigs. He wanted to get on the highway and never look back. Then you brought him into your world and fucked him up. Ruined him forever. Go home, Gedrin. You've got a tough forty-eight hours."

I wanted to stay and talk more shit, but my Jitterbug had other plans. It rang some weird tune and I realized it was Sims. I declined the call, but in an instant he'd texted me. *Thanks for the companions. Yours and hers tore up the furniture already.*

I laughed. I'd never told Sims about Mimi, but agents were good sleuths too.

"Your boy know I got a steel chin?" I said.

Nowa smiled. "It's glass, and he'll be ready."

Mimi walked out first, and Juko catcalled from the ring. She didn't turn around, just flicked him off while flexing her bicep.

I smiled, but I didn't look at Juko.

He'd get killed soon enough.

12

The next morning I woke up in a bed fit for multiple kings. Five-hundred-count Egyptian cotton tickled my ankles and a plush duvet warmed my shoulder blades. My head was sunk into a cool pillow. I was still team motel, but fight weekend was muy differente. No matter how much I tried to call all the shots, agents got one over on me sometimes. They were sticklers for details and they craved control the way an alcoholic craves the bottle. Sims wanted me close all fight weekend, and wouldn't you know it, he got his wish. I stretched full extension in the bed, expecting Henri to ruin the party at any moment.

But all was quiet.

I did three neck circles, and some of the pressure went away in the back of my head. It was a mirage of epic proportions, because that pressure would return full force in the ring with Juko. It'd call my name over and over again till I bested it or it bested me. For now though, I was excellente.

I hopped off the bed and checked myself out in the mirror. A weigh-in tradition. I turned left, right, forty-five degrees left, forty-five degrees right, and then I settled for straight-on. My abs were on point, and my muscles were thick slabs of steel. I couldn't remember what I ate last night, but in a few hours I'd be an encyclopedia.

Right after I made weight I'd get the hell out of Dodge. I'd tell Sims and Sal that I needed fresh air to clear my head. They'd want to go over game plans, but I'd want to go over menus. As in, which place on the Strip had the best stack of buttermilk blueberry pancakes. It'd be a rhetorical question, and when the team tried to answer it, I'd ignore them and go at it solo. Some things were best done in an individual capacity where nobody could ruin your rhythm. I'd find the perfect spot, and as an homage to Sal, I'd add protein powder to the batter for extra calories.

I examined my skin some more, poring over the pieces of involuntary body art that I'd picked up on the inside so many years ago. I closed my eyes and saw the bastard that had crossed me. The best medic in the world couldn't save his ass. Pride cometh before the fall. He learned, and Juko would too. I was part-destroyer, part-educator. I carried both titles with pride, and they never went out of style. Once I got in the zone, it was game over.

I smiled and went over the combos I'd throw in the fight. I closed my eyes and saw every last bit of it like a chessboard was clamped to my brain. I messed with my opponents in the opening seconds. I lulled them to sleep with simple jabs and right hands. Jab. Block. Jab. Block. Right. Back to defense. The problem was, Sal always wanted a clean first round, but I always wanted to *finish* it in the first round. It was a song and dance that started in our first fight and would most definitely go on till our last fight. I'd start Sal's way and then I'd go my way. I'd flip the switch. Combos galore. Left, body shot, uppercut. Right, left. Right hook. Body shot. And down goes Frazier. The order was more or less the same for every fight. Forward, backward, or something in-between. I didn't script the damned thing, but I sure as hell scripted the ending. To the victor go the spoils. I'd take the belt, cut a kickass promo that would make the Rock jealous, and I'd sing a tune for all the fans. If I had a guitar handy, I'd strum it loud and proud. When Sims didn't get me one in time, I'd strum an imaginary guitar. I was a jack of all trades. In all my years Sal sang the chorus with me only one time. "American Pie." The crowd ate the shit up, and so did the sponsors. The Benjamins flowed like candy and all was well with the world.

Juko would be no different.

The suits would open up their coffers, and I'd be back in the game, one step closer to the title I never lost. Maybe I'd get Sal to sing "American Pie" again or I'd tempt him with a new offering. The world was my oyster.

But one thing was certain. The titleholder would be ringside, flexing for the cameras. Sims had told me not to engage him after the fight, but he knew how the game was played. Hell yeah I'd engage the hombre. The more the merrier. I knew that once he saw me beat Juko's ass, he'd climb in the ring and act all hard. He'd talk shit for the cameras and I'd gladly give my response. But then the asshole would duck the title fight till the very last day he could defend it. Hell, he might even vacate the title to stay breathing. Self-preservation is a beautiful thing.

There was a knock at my door, and I wondered how Henri developed his manners so quickly.

Then a voice said, "Mr. Gedrin, sir?"

I told the voice to come in, and a housemaid greeted me. She bowed and blushed and asked if I wanted my clothes pressed for the weigh-in. I told her no, gracias, where's the perro? She laughed and said my Spanish was good and then said he was with the other perro.

Cool.

I thanked her, put my work clothes on, and went down a huge spiral staircase fit for the stars. On the road or at home, Sims lived in style. This rental had so many options it would take years to recite them all.

Sims was waiting for me at the kitchen island.

"Earth to the con," Sims said. He was wearing slim-cut jeans, a white polo, and a gold bracelet, and he had a headset in his ear. Just another day at the office.

"Hola," I said.

"What the hell are you wearing?" He glared at my purple sweats and "I Love Maple Syrup" t-shirt. He had an *I wanna have a heart attack* look. "Wear what the sponsors told you. You know the drill."

"The sponsors getting their brains beat in?" I said.

"They're signing on the dotted line, dammit."

I found my duffel bag on one of the counter stools and put a Nike hoodie over the shirt. Nike would get their time, but the syrup would too. Just wait.

Sims barked some orders into his headpiece for a couple minutes. Then he pushed a smoothie over to me and told me to drink it. I attacked it and wanted more, but there were greener pastures on the horizon.

Three minutes later Sims pressed a button on his ear and put his phone down. "Presser's gonna be so dope. They've got all the regulars, but national too. CNN. BBC. Fox. You can fucking sell a fight, what can I say?"

"You're welcome."

"By the way, your canine explosion last night cost me two grand for a new couch."

"Henri gets stressed in new environments," I said. "He got it from his mother."

Sims shook his head. "It was more the other behemoth than Henri. We adding girlfriends to the rock tour now?"

Sims always questioned my female companions. Never in the looks department, but always in the financial department. For him they were liabilities. Lawsuits waiting to bankrupt the bottom line. He gave me NDAs to give them, and I'd take them and rip them up when he wasn't looking. Sex and contracts were no bueno. But when these same female companions floated out of my life like a bout of influenza, Sims always had kind words. He'd pat my shoulder and say next time and she wasn't all that and you'll find the right one.

I said, "She's hanging out for the weekend."

"Good. Henri's taken to her. They're out on the town." He pushed a note over to me. It had female penmanship. *Chillin with the fur babies. C u later.* She left her number.

I wanted Mimi to see the weigh-in for the theatrics, but fur babysitting was important.

Sims went over strategy for the weigh-in. He gave me tips, tricks, and soundbites, and I nodded at all the right times and asked all the right questions at all the right moments. I'd ignore all of it when I was on stage, but now wasn't the time to spill.

Sims sensed something was up though. "We have a lot of security for this one," he said. "Don't go overboard."

"I want my corner protected," I said.

Sims shook his head. "Sal refuses a security detail and Leroy's gonna do whatever the hell Sal does."

"Figure it out. What the hell do I pay you for?"

I programmed Mimi's number into my Jitterbug and watched ESPN till my ride came.

Showtime.

13

And then there were four. Me, Sal, Leroy, and Bentini. All my seconds behind the curtain, waiting for me to make weight.

Sal said, "We'll get a couple of steaks after this."

I said, "Gotta cut the red."

Leroy said, "I want a Reuben, no sauerkraut."

Sal shook his head. "No sauerkraut, no Reuben. That's a tragedy, my man. Am I right, boyo?" He feigned a jab at me, then looked at Bentini for support.

The medical dressing over Bentini's ribs stuck out of the bottom of his shirt like a dilapidated pom-pom, but he'd sucked it up and made it to the weigh-in. His pops would have been proud. His sheer will motivated me to be better.

"Mustard makes the Reuben," Bentini said. "No contest." He stretched out and winced in pain. It'd be a while before all the parts worked again, but effort is the best word in town sometimes.

Sal feigned a heart attack and looked back at me for the

final word. As the employer of all these fine cornermen, I had a duty to settle all scores.

"A steak's a steak," I said. "But a Reuben's a Reuben. Apples and oranges."

Sal let it be, and I hopped on the floor and pumped out twenty pushups. The cameras wouldn't forget the gun show, and I wouldn't forget the cameras. When I got up, Sal went over some notes. While Sims was all about the PPV buys, Sal was all about the eyes. Don't blink first. Stare right through his skull. Show him who's champ. I didn't need any of the notes of course, but when Sal talked shop I listened—about fifty percent of the time. A legend's a legend.

I closed my eyes, and then Juko's name was announced to the crowd. He was stage left behind the curtain, while I was stage right. Our camps couldn't see each other, but in a few seconds we would. The crowd cheered, and I got butterflies for half a second. It'd been a while. But then it went away. Like riding a bike.

I was ready.

The announcer called my name next. The crowd had cheered Juko, but they blew the roof off the place with me. Sal tapped my shoulder and we all walked out on stage. The sharks were ready. Flash. Flash. Flash. *Mr. Gedrin!* Flash. Flash. Flash. *Juko sucks!* Flash. Flash. Flash. My pupils were lambasted with light, but all's fair in the fight game.

When I got up to the front, Juko's cronies formed a circle around him. Nowa must have been intimidated by *moi* because he'd hired seven bodyguards in addition to all the cornermen. He'd need a hell of a lot more to tame me. I looked at the ring girls, then at the canvas advertising the fight. I didn't care about the sponsors, but I cared about the font. My name was in Helvetica while Juko's was in Surfing Capital. I was the 'A' side, but I guess my legal disputes altered the execs' penmanship.

The announcer called Juko's name again, and he came out of the circle in his boxers. He walked onto the scale and stood there like a steel rod. The weight-checker hombre adjusted the weight-checker things and called out the weight.

Then the announcer said, "Two hundred twenty-seven pounds!"

Juko was too heavy to dance in the ring with me.

The announcer called my name again, and I went to work. The fight game is approximately twenty percent fight and eighty percent game. The game sold the t-shirts and the tickets and the Slurpees. The game gave you that mega green and that mega bling. Juko didn't know the game, but I was the Professor. Take notes.

I walked up to the middle of the stage, and Sal followed. I put my hand on his shoulder as I took off my black boots, my orange socks, and my purple sweats. I held my pose with the Nike hoodie for Sims, then I took it off and held my pose even longer with the "I Love Maple Syrup" tee. I stood there, soaking in the cheers and the boos and the catcalls from the ladies, then I took off the t-shirt too, and flung it to Sims. For an eternity I stood there in my boxers, and it was the best feeling in the world. Some things never get old. I did four neck circles and a fist pump, and then I hit the scale.

The weight-checker called the weight.

The announcer said, "Two hundred and three pounds!"

I wasn't done yet. The face-off was part of the fight game too. Juko was called up to center stage, and I made him wait. I put all my clothes back on, in reverse order. When I got to the hoodie, I tossed it into the press box for a souvenir. I could hear Sims shouting shit behind me. All in all, I took a minute flat to get dressed. Juko crinkled his nose.

We faced off.

Five seconds in, I shook my head and wagged my index fingers. Half the crowd booed, and the other half was confused. I looked at Sal, and he smiled. He reached into his bag and pulled out a red flat cap. He tossed it to me, and as a matter of courtesy I showed the crowd.

The cap read, *Juko's my bitch.*

The crowd went wild, and I put the cap on straight so Juko wouldn't feel left out.

Then all hell broke loose.

Just like I'd planned.

Juko pushed my chest.

I kicked his right knee.

Nowa pushed Sal.

Sal spit in Nowa's face.

Bodyguards held Juko back.

Leroy threw his water bottle at one of the cornermen, hitting him in the right eye socket.

I tossed a volunteer from Juko's camp like a rag doll.

Then I held the cap up to the crowd again. I had them eating out of my hand. The cameras flashed and the piece-of-shit Helvetica canvas crumpled behind me. Security eventually broke up the scrum.

But the weigh-in still wasn't over. We were contractually obligated to give a soundbite to the in-ring announcer. Short and sweet. He'd ask one question, and we'd each give one answer.

Juko first.

The announcer said, "What happened out there?"

Juko said, "That punk-ass Gedrin is gonna wish he was still locked up when I'm through with him. He's in for a long night."

The hombre was improving.

Juko and his team left the stage, and the announcer walked over to me.

"Gedrin, how's it feel to be back?"

I faced the cameras. "I'm not back till I get my damned title, which I never lost. To be the man, you gotta beat the man. But the problem is, I'm still the man. I can't fight myself. So I guess I'll settle for this kid Juko. He can come get it with the rest of his amateur-hour-fat-camp wannabes."

The crowd was one hundred percent behind me now.

Sal and the rest of the team went back to the locker room, and I stayed by the curtain to do press for a few more minutes. These were different outlets, and I wasn't required to speak to them, but I soaked it all in and enjoyed every last bit of it. I gave more detailed answers infused with more grit and wit. When I was done, I went back to the locker room.

But I couldn't get in.

A crowd was huddled around the door, whispering and crying. It brought me back to the zoo with Henri. A medic rushed out and another one rushed in.

And when the crowd parted, I saw Leroy on the ground with his eyes swollen shut. Blood had pooled around his head and vomit crusted his lips.

Bentini was sitting nearby, with a fresh injury. A medic was tending to a gash on the left side of his head. When he saw me, he gave me the kind of look that said our boy might not make it.

Another medic rushed in and they hoisted Leroy onto a stretcher. On their way out, one of the medics handed me a note. "This was hanging out of his pocket," he said. "Sorry, Gedrin. He's going to Desert Springs."

My mind was fried from cutting weight and all the other theatrics, but it didn't take a genius to see it.

Same word choice.

Same penmanship.

The note said: *1 Second Left.*

14

I ripped up the note and stormed outta there faster than a cheetah mid-stride. I took a right down the hall, a left, then another right. I learned early on in life that when the going got tough, my brain cells got going. I had no idea how many I had left after all my trials and tribulations, but boy did they fire when the moment called for it.

I went straight to the visitor's locker room. Where Juko and his punk-ass team were. They'd crossed the line, and I had no problem crossing it even more. Just bring it.

While the fight game was more game than fight, the minute a fighter let his emotions get the best of him, it was all over. Adios, amigos. For years, Sal would let me have it if I lost focus for even a minute. I prided myself on mental warfare. I was unflappable, unstoppable, undeniable. But Juko was winning that game now. Message sent, loud and clear. My ears were ringing, my head was in a vise, and my eyes were cloudy.

I was three feet away from the door, not a guard in sight. Now the fun would get real.

But I never made it.

Sims grabbed me by the collar and threw me up against the wall. He punched me twice in the stomach, knocking the wind out of me. Back in the day, before he got all fancy, Sims was an amateur fighter, and he could still throw down if need be. Not to the pro level, but respectable. What that meant in the grand scheme of things was that Sims could do damage with the right person at the right time. The average Joe on the street was toast. The pro, of course, would be fine—unless Sims had the element of surprise.

Which he had here.

"You fucking idiot," Sims said. "One step in there and you forfeit the fight. *And* your purse."

I pushed him off me and threw three jabs, but Sims dodged them all. We stared at each other for an eternity. He was my nemesis in that moment, and I'd destroy him to get what I wanted. Juko's head on a fucking spike. I would've sat there all day, but a shark dropped his camera down the hall, snapping me out of it. I looked at Sims again, and he relaxed. I followed suit, letting a stillness wash over my whole body. Option A was simple, but Option B was the better play. No way was I gonna lose my title shot.

Payback's a bitch. And I'd get mine soon enough.

Sims and I walked back toward the locker room.

"Where's Sal?" I asked.

"Outside. The whole place is locked down. Nobody in or out without ID. He was doing some blogger interview down the hall when it all went down."

"Show me the footage," I said.

"There's no surveillance. For privacy reasons. Showers and lockers and all that."

I didn't buy it for one second.

"Doesn't stop the sharks," I said.

Sims nodded. "They'll get him. He can run, but he can't

hide in this town. Somebody will fess up. Get your head in the game and let the chips fall into place."

I told Sims that the medics had taken Leroy. He blasted the keys on his phone and made a few calls. When we got back to the locker room, yellow caution tape barricaded the entrance and Bentini was giving a statement to some stadium cops. They hadn't worked a case of this magnitude before and it showed. Once the big guns came in to take the reins, they'd be pushed aside.

One second left.

The note couldn't have been more clear.

First Bentini.

Then Leroy.

Sal was next.

My corner was falling to the wolves twenty-four hours before my comeback fight.

Sims got off the phone and turned to me. "No interviews about this. Not a fucking word. Let's go."

"It'll be a feeding frenzy," I said.

"Mandy says business as usual. Control the narrative and don't let the narrative control you. No letup. The sponsors are gonna eat that shit up when you get in the ring tomorrow and take care of business."

Mandy was my old publicist. Sims had had her on payroll from my very first pro fight, and she coordinated all my TV appearances and interviews. Sims took the credit for his Benjamins, but the truth was, he had Mandy to thank for the vast majority of them. And both of them had *me* to thank for the whole enchilada. Without their moneymaker, they knew where they'd be. I hadn't seen Mandy in thirteen years, but she knew the game.

"And what if Juko kicks my ass?" I said.

Sims paused.

Then we both busted out laughing.

Losing wasn't an option.

As we continued down the hall, Sims got back on his phone. We ran into Sal, who stopped me.

"Those *pendejos* are gonna get a taste of their own medicine," he said.

"Where were you?" I said.

"Flora Munoz. *Fight Weekly*. She wanted the whole story. From the brass knucks to Goluka to now."

I appreciated the nostalgia and Sal promoting the brand, but I also appreciated bodily preservation.

"You're staying with me tonight," I said. "They're coming for you next."

"Who?" Sal said.

"The assholes who tuned up Leroy and Bentini."

Sal crinkled his nose. "They want some, they gotta come get some. Can't hit what you can't see, boyo." He held his hands up and threw a few jabs.

Sal and I were different in many respects, but alike in others. During times of strife we laughed everything off. We didn't believe what we should've believed. We were too stubborn for our own good. And we had one solution to solve all our ills.

Kick the person's ass who caused you harm.

I said, "You'll never learn."

"That makes two of us. I wouldn't have it any other way." He threw some more jabs, and I blocked them. "Good. More. The kid over there's not as shitty as you think."

"But his trainer is."

We shared a laugh and threw some more combinations in the hallway. Sal threw jabs, rights, uppercuts, left hooks, right hooks, body shots. He wasn't wearing any mitts, and I wasn't wearing any padding. If I slipped up, I'd get a legit shot. He'd put me on a stretcher right before my fight, and all Sims's connects couldn't save me. But I didn't slip up, and I didn't take a shot. I was ready.

Sal was ready, too. And Bentini was semi-ready.

But Leroy... he was fighting for his life.

A part of me wanted to cancel the fight out of respect. But another part of me understood the reality of this business. The show must go on. If I didn't fight, contracts would be violated and lawyers would make a fortune and fans would turn.

And Leroy's family wouldn't get paid a dime.

Nobody in my corner would.

So the game was on, and unfinished business was unfinished business. Maybe not today, maybe not tomorrow, but I'd find out who'd roughed up my seconds. I'd search long and far and wide. I'd ruffle all the right feathers in all the right caps. And when I got to the bottom of it, the notemaker would be in a body bag faster than you can say hola.

I'd zip it up real nice and put a bow on it. Then I'd throw it in the river and never look back.

Sal got me with a body shot.

"Damn, boyo. Come on!" Sal shook his head and threw another hard body shot, even harder. I blocked it, and we were back in business. Left. Right. Left. Right. Slip. It was poetry in motion. Boxing was muy bueno.

Then Sal got tired and I got hungry.

One of the stadium cops asked for a statement, but Sims did his lawyer talk and I was free.

I wasn't in the mood to find a place, so I told him to tell the chef at the house to make pancakes. For performance-enhancing benefits. Sims nodded and got back on his phone.

When I looked behind me, Sal was gone.

15

Mimi had two flapjacks, and I had seven. I was in Heaven with all the maple syrup. Henri sat at my knees and Bruce sat at hers.

"What do you feed this monster?" Mimi said. "He was pulling like a Siberian Husky on the slopes."

I looked down at Henri, who was slobbering on a duck biscuit. "In times of stress, Henri enjoys excessive cardiovascular activity."

Mimi laughed. "Bruce almost copy-catted, but he stayed with his momma."

"He's got a nice momma."

"Thanks."

"She has a good heart."

Mimi blushed a little, then went back to her plate. It was empty and had been for several minutes, but maybe she was pondering another stack of flapjacks. When the mind wanted sugary goodness, the synapses didn't fire straight.

I, on the other hand, was just getting started. I grabbed three more flapjacks, a ham and cheese omelet, and a big glass of OJ. Henri begged, but I was in the zone. See food, eat food. Rinse and repeat. The Monday-morning quarterbacks always talked shit about my diet whenever things didn't go my way in the ring. Which was about as rare as a bag of purple carrots. They theorized that sugar destroyed my mojo. I theorized that sugar gave me an edge. I was wired all day, and when I climbed in the ring I was extra wired.

Mimi said, "Don't your trainers force raw eggs down your throat?"

I said, "They make me squeamish."

"Rocky didn't mind."

I had no comeback there. The cinema works wonders. It illuminates the ups and downs of certain segments of society and takes a profession and dissects it better than the best surgeon in the land. Doctor. Lawyer. Boxer. You name it, the cinema has portrayed it. For better or worse. The fight game left an inedible mark on the world, and being a part of it meant knowing all the cinematic lore. I loved Rocky.

I went back to my pancakes, and my mind went back to Leroy. I wanted to visit him in the hospital, but Sims said he was in a coma—and Sims wanted me a million miles away from his hospital bed. No fucking around on the eve of the fight. I felt like a loser boss, but I took solace in the fact that Leroy would probably pull through. If he were really in danger, even Sims would break rules and tell me to get my ass over there to be by his side.

Mimi must have read my thoughts. "Sorry about your friend," she said. "They'll catch the dude. They always do."

"I certainly hope so. For their sake."

"That sounds like a threat."

"You lawyers have a lot of brain cells."

I smiled, and Mimi returned it. I petted Henri and gave

him another duck biscuit. Bruce stared me down like I had the plague, then he rolled over on his side.

"He's hurt," Mimi said.

"I should've got the jumbo bag."

Mimi petted Bruce's belly, and he closed his eyes and drifted to sleep. "How does someone get inside an arena with all that security and do something like that?" she asked.

I'd gone over the scenarios in my head the way I went over the tape of my opponents in the ring. I'd dissected every angle, looked at every nuance, peeked at every nook and cranny. And it all came back to the same inescapable conclusion.

Somebody on the inside.

Mowing down my seconds.

Some guard, janitor, or media hombre granted access, and the notemaker did his thing. Or her thing, though based on the penmanship I doubted the maker was female.

"There's no surveillance in the locker room," I said.

"The old privacy stonewall," Mimi said. "Nothing some finely crafted subpoenas won't fix."

"Speak subpoena to me, missy."

Mimi grinned. "They'll pull that feed from the locker room faster than you could say *corpus delicti*."

"Damn."

Mimi was good.

Mimi said, "Any lawyer worth his salt sends the subpoena or the FOIA, it's game over."

"Doesn't matter," I said. "They won't find shit on that tape."

"Why?"

"Because I have a hunch."

"You know what they say about hunches?" Mimi said.

"I sure do."

Mimi told me anyway. "They're like assholes."

"Ewww," I said.

Mimi punched me. That made two punches since she'd met me. Things were looking way up.

"Things always work out in the end," she said. "I've seen shit that I wouldn't wish on my worst enemy. Like this seven-year-old boy who got saved from a burning house up in Brighton. Total feel-good story, right? Nope. Grandma tossed him out the window to his mama, but Grandma didn't make it out. And that's not all. After, they check up on the kid. Mama says her story. The kid repeats Mama's story. Then they see the bruises and the cigarette marks on his back. The cuts above his dick. They take the kid aside and he spills. Mama was beating the kid, and on that one night, the kid was back with Grandma while Mama went on a date. The kid was in a safe place for the first time in his life, and look what happened. Some people are pure evil. Bad apples. The nature of the beast. But they all get their just deserts sooner or later."

Mimi had tears in her eyes.

"They can run, but they can't hide," I said. "When I get something in my head, I never let it go. I chase it down till chasing goes out of style. I take no prisoners. I win, they lose." I got out of my chair and gave Mimi a hug. She never asked for it, but sometimes you take a chance and let the chips fall where they may.

They fell my way all right.

Mimi fell into my arms and cried. We held each other, and I didn't want it to stop.

But all good things come to an end.

Mimi broke away.

"You're making me sappy," she said.

"Not in a million years."

"Get your head in the game. I don't like mingling with knockout recipients."

GREG GOUNTANIS

"I'm a giver, not a receiver."

Mimi shook her head. "You're so bad. I like it."

We stood there for a few more seconds, Mimi examining the square footage of the place, and me examining the last sausage link on my plate. Then I attacked it and Henri barked his appreciation.

"How many calories did you just ingest?" Mimi asked, hands on hips.

"Mucho," I said.

"Those poor arteries."

"A breakfast of champions a day keeps the doctor away."

Mimi shook her head and let Bruce out onto the patio. Henri followed. They stood at attention like they were at Navy SEAL BUD/S training.

"They are so cute together," Mimi said.

"It takes two to tango."

"Agreed." And then Mimi took my hand and did a pirouette. She showed me dance moves I didn't know existed. We waltzed and danced and looked like complete amateurs. When it was all over, I was speechless. Mimi wasn't.

"Not bad for a newb," she said.

"Teach me more."

She smiled. "Okay."

But then, Mimi's phone rang. Mimi answered and said a bunch of legal things I didn't understand. When she was done, she looked like she'd seen a ghost.

"I have to get back to Portland," she said. "Big case coming in. I can't say more."

I said nothing.

74

16

An hour later, Mimi was in an Escalade. Sims had one on standby, complete with his own personal driver, and I used it whenever my heart desired. Chivalry is a beautiful thing. Mimi and I sat in the back, with Bruce between us. His head touched the ceiling, but he didn't complain one bit. If only Henri had that kinda discipline.

The driver took the busiest freeway at the busiest time of the day, and we were soon clumped together with the rest of the steel masses of commerce. Smog and exhaust and horns and rubber. Bruce must have picked up on the cues because he looked over at me, snorted, and drooled on my thigh. Then he lay down, invading my space.

"Henri's gonna miss his furry friend," I said.

"Bruce doesn't like to show empathy, but behind closed doors he's game," Mimi said. She patted Bruce's head and looked out her window at a horse trailer in the next lane. The slats were small but any average Joe could see those horse snouts sticking out. Plus there was the olfactory explosion that wafted our way.

I sighed and settled in for the long haul. I folded my legs like a pretzel, leaned back against the headrest, closed my eyes, and pictured Juko getting his brains beat in. The synapses combusting like soggy French fries. The eyes cracking like peanuts. Seeing is believing. The fight was over in my mind before it ever started. The devil's in the details. I had no idea what other fighters thought about, but it didn't matter.

They weren't up to my level.

The driver slammed the brakes, and my head bounced off the headrest. He swore at the cabbie in front and apologized on his behalf. If Mimi and I got to our destination *sans* injury, I would judge today a good day.

"Thanks for the weekend," Mimi said. She was still looking out the window. "Who knew a stranger could be so awesome?"

"When you meet a pretty lady at the zoo, you can't let the moment pass."

"Aw, cute. Your dimples are showing."

"Not a chance."

"Gotcha." Mimi punched me again. That made three punches since the zoo.

"Owee."

I was silent after that. Mimi too. We sat there like our mouths were stuck in cement. Two strangers in an escalade with a Great Dane keeping them company. I wanted to peek into her brain and get to the bottom of it all. But courtship was a strange beast.

Then it hit me.

Lawyer talk.

The suits couldn't resist it, and they craved it like a junkie craved the needle. Part therapy and part emesis.

I said, "OJ won the case fair and square."

Mimi looked away from the window. "Really."

"The jury saw all the police shenanigans and forensic fuckups. They had to acquit. If it doesn't fit you must acquit."

"Motive was there. Science had his name on it, despite the mirage with the collection efforts. Blood in the socks. His. Bloody glove. His. Witnesses put him driving away frantically from the scene around the timeline of the murder. Whaddya say about that, mister?"

"Reasonable doubt is reasonable doubt."

Mimi laughed. "You, sir, should have been a lawyer."

"I'm allergic to owing the government funds."

Mimi smiled. "If they want you, it's over."

"In a heartbeat. How many doozy cases you have?"

"What?"

"Whoppers. The big kahunas. Stylin' and profilin'."

The lawyer talk was working beautifully.

Mimi shrugged. "Depends. If you're talking first-chair, leading the whole thing? Zero. I'm not assigned to homicides. If you're talking carrying the briefcase, doing some witnesses, I've second-chaired a shitload. Beats my robberies and thefts and fraud dudes any day of the week."

"So they're calling you back for the big stuff."

Mimi said nothing.

I knew lawyers had their whole privilege fascination, but I was curious. What had ruined our weekend? What was drawing her away that couldn't wait till Monday? What made her wanna miss me kicking Juko's candy ass?

I waited Mimi out, and finally she cracked. "I'm not at liberty to say. But it's big, or they wouldn't be calling a government employee on a weekend."

"The struggle is real," I said. "You can slip it to Bruce, and I'm mum."

"I wish."

Damn.

The suits were anal about the details.

I considered annoying Mimi some more, but I let it be. She looked out the window again and I followed suit on my side. The horse trailer had crossed multiple lanes and I could see all the snouts now. Then the trailer changed lanes back toward us, dust filled the air, and the olfactory explosion said hello again.

"Make sure you beat the case," I said.

"Easier said than done."

"Cool."

Mimi looked over at me. "Sorry about my callousness. I'm devoid of emotions sometimes. How much time did you do anyway?"

"Mucho."

"You have the con walk."

"A top-notch one."

Mimi laughed. "It's quite distinctive. It's almost like a limp and a hitch and a gallop at the same time."

"I've got more distinctive attributes." I grinned.

"Yeah? I'm surprised you can function in that ring." She grinned.

"Missy, you are bad."

Mimi looked at Bruce and he looked at her sideways. Then he looked at me sideways. Then he barked at the horse trailer changing lanes again. Apparently nobody gave citations in Vegas these days.

"Keep working on that jab," I said. "You have what it takes."

"I think I'll stick to my day job. I like jabbing chubby prosecutors with my words."

"Working the maxilla is muy bueno."

"Again with the Spanish," Mimi said.

"Force of habit."

"Tell me more."

"No way, Jose. Security clearance is real."

Mimi shook her head. "And to think I got stood up on a first date."

"The world's a cruel place, señora. Lot of bad hombres out there."

"What are *hombres*?"

"People."

"That's what I thought." Mimi looked back out the window. "I've never had somebody be so chill around me. Somebody always wants something. In the courtroom. In my personal life. I really appreciate it. Truly."

"No prob."

We were approaching the airport. The driver said, "Terminal?"

Mimi told him, and two minutes later we were there. The driver unloaded Bruce's cage and Mimi's one bag. He shut the trunk, said some pleasantries, and went back to the car. Bruce would have to curl up in that cage at some point, but he still had time before check-in. Poor boy.

Now came the moment of truth.

There came a time in every platonic friendship where the male or the female would make their true intentions known. One party would move their maxilla and the other would take it all in. If maxilla man picked up on all the right signs at all the right times, it'd be a match. Platonic friendship no more. If not, it'd be a long ride out of Dodge filled with lingering questions.

Mimi moved her maxilla first.

"We should do this again sometime," she said. "Jitterbug man."

I said nothing.

I didn't need to.

Mimi leaned in and kissed me. And then, leash in hand, she was gone.

Platonic friendship no more.

17

I didn't tell Sal. As much as he liked gossip, he liked solitude more. During fight week he always crashed at the best motel in the best part of town. Away from all the noise and all the hoopla. While the average person couldn't get enough of the glitz, Sal plopped on his flimsy bed and did what every trainer worth his salt did: he went to film school. He pulled out every tape known to man and dissected it like a heart surgeon. He stood there for hours braving styes and cataracts, all because he knew the reality. Fighters win fights, but trainers lose them. Turnover was part of the job. Lose a fight and you'll be out on your ass faster than you can say hola. At least that's how it worked with other camps. Before I came along. Sal held that PTSD like a crutch and never let me forget it.

Fight eve meant fight school.

Sal called me right after my non-platonic smooch with Mimi and told me where he was staying. I re-routed the Escalade, and we hit no traffic on the way back. His motel was a purple- paint-lined bundle of joy that should have been repainted decades ago. Two floors with five rooms on each. An ice machine on one and a soda machine on two. Sal didn't tell me the room number, but as soon as I got out he hollered from a second-floor unit.

"Boyo! Move your ass! That shit won't fly tomorrow!"

So much for laying low with a dude mowing down all my seconds.

As much as I wanted to throw it all in the rearview mirror and focus on the fight, I could picture Leroy's family at his funeral. All the tears and whispers and cries and pointed fingers. I was guilty by association. I'd allowed it all to happen. My fight, my drama. And if Leroy didn't make it out of his coma, it'd be on *my* head. On the outside, grief slid off me like I was Teflon, but inside was a whole other ballgame.

I'd fought a thousand wars, from the time Mama Gedrin kicked the bucket to now, and I'd come out on top each time. But my world drew the crazies. My whole life was a shit show, and would continue to be a shit show. Still, I wouldn't have it any other way. I relished the chaos. And I wouldn't rest till I got answers. For Leroy. For Bentini. For Sal. Though the geriatric asshole was probably good. He'd either knock his way out of harm's way or annoy the shit out of the notemaker till he quit.

I thanked the driver for his services and walked up the steps. I could feel Sal's eyes on me like molten lava ready to erupt. He was the best damned trainer in the business, but that didn't mean I was playing patsy. I stopped at the soda machine, put in some quarters, shook the machine when my beverage got stuck, and pulled it out.

"You're giving me another bypass!" Sal shouted.

I smiled and walked down the floor to his unit. When I reached him, I held the bottle up for inspection.

"Bottled water, boyo? How many times I tell you to drink straight from the tap? Don't be foolish with your money."

"I have plenty," I said.

"You have shit," Sal said. "You blow this fight and they'll tie the purse up in court for years. The lawyers know all the loopholes."

"Technicalities are the best game in town."

"Maybe that Simba can figure it out." He was talking about Sims. Some days he called him Sims, other days he called him Simba. Maybe the cumulative effect of punches was finally taking its toll. I wanted to tell him that Simba ended up king of the jungle. *Hakuna matata.* But I let it slide.

"He's already figured it out," I said.

"He better. The missus don't like no bouncy checks. And my stupid son too. Can barely keep the gym alive."

Sal let me inside and a cacophony of photos greeted me. They were spread out all over the bed like a rainbow. Juko in the ring in a bunch of different poses. Jab. Left hook. Covering up. In the corner. Right hook. I knew the photographer. I called him Numero Uno. He took the finest shots over the years and sold them to the finest magazines. And apparently Sal was in on the gig too. He had Uno's finest collections.

"Some side hustle," I said.

Sal whacked me over the head with his palm. "Keep talking down your opponent and see what he's gonna do tomorrow. This ain't a press conference, boyo. Sit."

There weren't any chairs in the room, but Sal had other plans. He pointed to a piece of construction paper with a big 'X' on it.

"You sit. You listen," he said. "You've been outta the game so long, we've had three presidents."

I said, "It's all Greek to me."

"Juko's a southpaw. He likes to set the jab early, and when he has you in the clinch he's gonna get as many cheap shots in as he can. He'll lose the points but wear you down and take you in the tenth."

Sal showed me some photos of Juko in the clinch. I nodded like I was very into Sal's presentation. It was a matter of appearances, but appearances mattered in the fight game. Respect your elders. When Sal talked shop, I listened in one ear and misinterpreted and misapplied out the other.

I knew my game plan.

Kick Juko's ass. Walk him down and take him out early. Fuck the tenth.

Sal took another picture off the bed. "Nowa's never gonna throw in the towel. When you go for the body shot and uppercut, you'll catch air. I've been watching them. He fought Anton last fight. Made him look like stale cheese. He set it all up in camp. He's a machine."

"What kind of cheese?" I said.

"Swiss."

"Snitches get stitches."

Sal smiled. "I paid some junior to video the camp. Nobody says shit when a kid goes in there and wants pictures and videos for the internet. Everybody wants to be a virus these days."

"You mean viral?"

Sal shook his head. "Virus, viral. Tomato, tomahto."

He pulled out his phone and showed me the clip. The kid held a steady frame, and Sal was right: Juko was in fine form. He was sparring with a behemoth who threw all my favorite combinations. Juko blocked every one. At one point he knocked the behemoth down and they replaced him with another behemoth. Juko knocked his ass down too. He made mincemeat of Anton a few days later. The tape ended, and Sal was all smiles.

"You love a challenge," I said.

"If there's no blood, it ain't a fight, boyo."

I looked over the photos and catalogued them in my brain. I was a computer with unlimited memory, even if I was smidgen older and slower. When the time came I'd put everything together and get the job done. Ring rust sucked, but come tomorrow it'd be like I'd never left.

Sal turned the TV on and stuck a USB on the side of it. The motel really was something.

"How many channels you got?" I said.

"One." Sal pressed a few buttons. "My son is good for one thing at least." He hit the remote, and Juko appeared on the screen. Nowa was in his corner with another trainer and another cutman.

I watched for a few minutes, taking mental notes.

Then my mind went back to Nowa.

"How'd your old friend Nowa take the ass-kicking today?" I said.

Sal shook his head. "Good play with the cap. That bitch didn't want any of this. I wanted to finish what I started, but I lost the asshole in the scrum."

Or maybe Nowa was back in our locker room, lying in wait for his prey.

I watched a couple more minutes of film, and then Sal played good cop for a change.

"Get some sleep, boyo. You're almost back to the top of the mountain."

18

I took a cab back to good ole Flamingo Road. I knew the landmarks better than the lines on my hand, and the ride was smooth. The cabbie talked politics and I talked casinos. Then the cabbie talked casinos and I talked politics. We droned on for thirty-three minutes and would have droned on for many more if it wasn't for the scorpion in the road. Life wasn't like the movies, but this time it was. When the cabbie saw the scorpion, he jerked the steering wheel to the left and the front wheels careened off some needles on the pavement before making music with a guardrail. The scorpion survived the near homicide, but the cab didn't. Two flats and a front fender that looked like a dilapidated horse's hoof.

"Just my luck," the cabbie muttered.

"It must be a sign," I said.

The cabbie raised his brows. Then he seized his opening and talked marital infidelity and religion and shame. I nodded at all the right moments and gave my two cents worth at all the others. I wasn't a counselor by any means, but sometimes you gotta fake it till you make it. It went like that till a green tow truck showed up. All four corners of the truck said "Lenny's" with a font that looked more crayon than Courier. The decals were frayed and next month Lenny would need new decals. Till then he could keep busy and wipe the truck bed one hundred times and fix the bullet hole in the front passenger window.

A burly man in carpenter's jeans and construction boots stepped out. He looked like he'd fixed a lotta cars in his time, and fucked up a lot of cars too. I presumed the man was Lenny, but things are stranger than fiction sometimes.

The cabbie said, "One large flat. Driver side."

"And the fender's no bueno," I said. "Lenny?"

"Wrong. I been wondering he at meself," the man said. He had an Irish accent and right then I knew Lenny owned the shop while the man that came out to fix all this shit courtesy of the scorpion got none of the credit.

The man went back to his truck, reversed it, and lined it up with the cab. He got out to line up all the rods and poles and things, but the cabbie stopped him.

"You have another spare, I can fix it and be on my way. Don't need to trouble you any more tonight."

The man snorted. "What a bunch of bollocks. I look like a franchise to you?"

The cabbie said nothing.

"Size seventeen," I said. "Thirty-five PSI. There's one in back." I pointed to the prize on the truck nestled between some paint buckets. I'd taken a class back in high school and could talk shop with the best of them. I was the Professor and wasn't about to give up my crown.

"No tread," the man said.

We were at a crossroads. If the cabbie insisted on no tread, we'd swing a deal and be on our merry way. If not, we'd watch as the Irishman left with the cab and the scorpion avoided another homicide. Then we'd make a call for a ride. And I might never get to my destination. My battery was running low, and the Jitterbug was really sensitive. Hopefully the cabbie had some juice.

"To the victor go the spoils," I said.

The cabbie looked confused. The Irishman too.

"No tread, no prob," I said. "We fix it, you tell Lenny to stop getting shit from those secondhand shops."

The Irishman laughed. "This codger." He took the spare from the truck bed and rolled it to me. I then rolled it to the cabbie, and he went to work. I analyzed the cabbie's form, and the Irishman did too. The cabbie struggled with the jack, and at one point I was tempted to lend a helping hand, but if at first you don't succeed, try, try again.

I saw the Irishman eyeing me. "You look familiar," he said.

I shrugged. "I get mistaken for famous sleuths all the time."

"No, I seen you on the TV."

The cabbie looked up at me. "The meter's still running, Hollywood."

I put my hands up and said, "These hammers don't lie."

The Irishman laughed, and the cabbie too. If the scorpion hadn't hightailed it out of Dodge, he'd have joined all the mirth.

When the tire was finally on, the Irishman asked for an autograph, and I obliged. I told him to scold Lenny about the paint job, and then he was gone.

The cabbie made it to the gym seven minutes later. I tipped him more than respectably and went inside.

What a difference a day makes.

No Mimi.

No nine-to-five crowd.

No Nowa.

And no Juko.

I scanned the gym and saw one young up-and-comer

working the heavy bag. He had a mean left hook but a wobbly right. Nowa was spending too much time in front of the cameras and not enough time educating the masses. It rubbed me the wrong way. The fight game was all about education. Sal did it with the best of them. Nowa was an asshole who was probably mowing down my seconds or at the very least knew who was. He should've forgotten his crimes of collusion and focused on the youth. The youth spread the word and put in the work and let the gym live on for generations. Set aside the fancy leather and the fancy lights and the fancy ring, and at the end of the day 'twas a people's game.

I walked up to the kid, who did a double-take when he saw me. Then he did a half bow and couldn't stop smiling.

"Show me that right," I said.

The kid got nervous, then he composed himself and threw a few rights. Each more wobbly than the one before.

"Put your legs into it and snap it." I showed the kid. He tried it and failed. Then he tried it again and failed again. Then he tried it one more time and failed one more time. But less of a failure than before.

"It feels weird," he said.

"Muscle memory," I said. "Keep working it and it'll be like riding a bike. How long you been at it?"

"Eight months."

"Damn. You have potential."

The kid beamed. "Hava keeps ignoring me. No matter what I do."

"He's a bitch. Take anything he says with three grains of salt. You put in the work, you'll get there. You don't need this fancy shit. See it. Punch it. Commit."

The kid nodded. "Are you nervous about Juko?"

I smiled. "The only thing I'm nervous about is if they run outta pancakes for my post-fight celebration."

The kid laughed. "You're something."

"Speaking of the bitch, where's Hava at? I wanna talk a little shit to him before tomorrow."

The kid shook his head. "Place has been dead since five. He came here with Juko, talked a little to the cameras, then they left."

"Together?"

"No. Juko went home. Hava kept saying he was gonna have some fun before the big night. Then the place cleared out like an apocalypse, man."

I smiled. "I'm in his head."

"I'll say. Where'd you get that hat? I wanna tell my friends I got the champ-champ's hat."

"I'll do you one better," I said. "What's your number?"

The kid gave it to me and I told him I'd get him tickets for the fight.

Pays to have a good agent.

19

I still wasn't sleepy. I got an Uber with durable tires this time. The driver didn't ask many questions and I didn't give many answers. I told her my destination and I got crickets the rest of the way. Maybe it was where I was going or maybe it was the silence of sharing a car with a stranger when a full moon peeked out over the canyons. Both were equally plausible, but I leaned toward the former.

It was Nowa who made me do it. Follow me. He was having fun before the fight, and I would too. The kid at the gym didn't need to tell me the exact spot. Any person with half a toupee could figure it out.

You want fun in Nevada? Follow me.

The Uber driver gripped the steering wheel the way an anaconda does its prey. She wore a Seattle Seahawks jersey and black jeans. She had black curls and a nose ring. I pegged her for university age, hustling multiple gigs to make ends meet. Hell, she might have gluten-free pizzas in the trunk and I was messin' with her route. I smiled, and she caught me in her rearview.

"What's your problem?" she said.

"I'm sensitive to hydrogen peroxide. Damn the pearly whites." I showed them to her and her nose ring almost killed me.

I went back to the window and she went back to the road. Traffic was nonexistent and I vowed right there to give her all the stars. I didn't know how many the Uber system had, but whatever it was I'd give it, no problemo. My last two drivers had elevated my blood pressure far too many points and I needed respite. But then again, Mimi was with me for part of the previous rides, so there was that.

What a counselor.

I closed my eyes and listened to her voice. Sweet, charming. Soothing like aloe vera gel. And with a nice dose of sass. Just the way I liked it. I thought I wanted something substantive, but she'd made it clear that that wasn't in the cards anymore. Chicago made me jaded, but the turn of the tide is really something. I wanted to whip out the Jitterbug and send a witty line, but not right now. Texting across states at this late hour communicated one thing and one thing only: hunger. I'd be knocked outta the game faster than you can say Juko. I had to play my cards right and make my move *after* the fight. That was the best way to go about it. Play it cool and take everybody to school. I wasn't an expert by any means, but stubbornness was my middle name. Once I took Nowa and Juko to school, I'd profess my feelings for her right in the ring. I'd serenade her from nine hundred miles away with the whole world watching.

Take that, Casanova.

I watched the valleys and the windmills coming out of hibernation. The humidity seeped through the windows and stuck to my shirt. Just another Nevada night.

Three minutes later we reached our destination. A fuchsia-lit sign beckoned consumers forward and teased them with more to come. The Seahawks girl crinkled her nose as she parked.

"Couples get a discount," I said.

"La-di-da," she said.

"Over-under six pepperonis."

"What?"

I pointed at the pizza slice decoration hanging from her rearview. "How many you delivering?"

"Not enough to pay child support." She checked the stability of her nose ring and flared her nostrils.

"Give me carbs or give me death," I said as I got out.

And just like that, she was gone. The car screeched away and I walked past the fuchsia signage into the Toots Life brothel.

The place was a stalwart in the pleasure business. With prostitution illegal in all of the United States except for some collar Nevada counties, Toots Life made bank off of the fantasies and eccentricities of its clientele. Doctors, lawyers, garbage men, celebrities, fiddlers. Fun played no favorites, but it sure played your pocketbook. And with an HBO special a few years back featuring all the quirks of all the working girls, the place charged premium price for premium experience.

Couples got a discount.

Too bad Nowa and I weren't at that stage in our relationship.

When I crossed the threshold into the main parlor, the dim lights put me in a dungeon and gave me a ginormous migraine. So much for the PTSD going away after all these years. The madam of the house made small talk with me and led me into another room with a long plush couch. I sat down and waited. I knew the procedures like the back of my hand. Sal might have been a stickler for pancakes pre-fight, but he was far more liberal post-fight. After I won my first title, Sal shuttled half the team to Toots Life, and I'd be lying if I said it wasn't muy bueno.

The madam rang the bell.

Showtime.

The ladies came out in heels and robes and bonnets and trinkets and more. But not too much more. They walked past me and formed a single-file line. Then they all said their names, one by one, twirling after the last syllable came out and smiling wider than the *Mad Magazine* poster boy. Much had changed over the years, and for the better. Not only were the girls from all sorts of racial backgrounds, but geographic backgrounds too. Spain. Italy. Brazil. Myrtle Beach. Harbor Town. Boston. South Dakota. St. Paul. Chicago. Athens.

I was tempted to ask the Chicago girl twenty-one questions to assess her credibility, but I could only think of three.

I went with the Athens girl. She called herself Magrece and had long green curls, one pierced earlobe, and an ass that put me to shame any day of the week. She was five-ten and had probably never eaten a French fry in her life. Or looked at one. The other gals left, the madam smiled, and Magrece led me by the hand to the back.

For the tour.

Standard procedure. Once the customer chooses his gal for the evening, sly tactics ensue. This was a business after all. One that had gone on since the beginning of time and would surely go on till the end of time. Magrece showed me the bar and the pool and the ping-pong table and the mystery zone and then the bedroom. She highlighted all the pros of all the spots and glossed over all the cons. She was a natural.

She closed her door and led me to the bed.

"How are you feeling today, handsome?" She rubbed my shoulders and worked her way up to my ears.

"Betrayed," I said. "By an old friend."

If Magrece was surprised by the bullshit I was spewing, she didn't show it. She went back to my shoulders. If she decided to hit my pec minor next, I'd be laughing like a hyena. I was ticklish.

"Honey, what do you need?"

"A little bit of Hava and a little bit of Nowa." I hadn't seen or heard the bastard so far, but the gals worked together. Discretion was the name of the game in parts like this, and if Nowa was in the mystery zone nobody'd be the wiser.

Magrece worked her way down from my shoulders to my chest to my belly. She undid my shirt. No tickles there.

"Mr. Muscles over here," she said. "Do you like when I call you that, honey?" She tossed the shirt and went for my belt.

"The name's Pancho. Pancho Villa."

Magrece smiled. "Pancho, you're making me wet." She ignored my belt for a moment and I had no complaints. She took her bra off and then her panties. I still had no complaints.

"What are you gonna do to me, Pancho?"

"Can I have a menu?"

On a normal day with a normal woman in a normal bedroom in a normal world, I'd have killed the mood. But pleasure and commerce make strange bedfellows.

"Missionary," Magrece said. "Doggy. Piledriver. Deep throat. Double trouble. Anal's triple. Stratusfaction. A la carte."

I said, "No satisfaction?"

Magrece told me the difference, and it all made sense.

I had a tough decision to make. On the one hand, I wanted to wax poetic about all the gaps in the menu and make suggestions accordingly. On the other hand, I'd come here for a reason.

"A la carte," I said.

I told her what I wanted.

In detail.

Then came price. The best negotiators in the world didn't live in courtrooms or boardrooms. Nope. The best were in the bordellos. Magrece could drive a hard bargain with her eyes closed.

She gave a number and I countered with a number. Then she countered with another number and the song and dance went on for two minutes and thirty-eight seconds.

Then I'd had enough.

I said, "I want to pay what Hava Nowa paid."

And then Magrece had had enough.

She slapped the shit out of me, and I noticed something that wasn't there the last time I was at Toots Life.

A big red panic button.

Magrece hit it. And the cavalry came.

20

A skinny man in a cowboy hat was numero uno. He had a porn-star mustache and a soiled button-down that was tucked in way past its expiration date. One's a crowd, but trouble comes in twos and threes and fours. The panic button was a clever invention. Protect the working girls. Get the cash. Any hombre dumb enough to provoke the situation deserved all the trouble that came next. That would teach him a lesson for next time. Fail to contribute to the machine and go down like a bag of rocks.

Unfortunately for the faithful at Toots, I loved trouble. I ate a dose of it for breakfast, lunch, and dinner and always left room for dessert. I never got full. Life was better lived on the edges. More tiempo to enjoy it all. More tiempo to make memories. More tiempo to break records.

Damned good ones.

But I was off this time.

Trouble came in sixes and sevens.

The cowboy man smiled and fanned out to my left. Then the room filled with seven Mr. Olympia hopefuls who would never reach the stage. They formed a semicircle around me and cracked their knuckles. The buildup to a fight was my absolute favorite. Oxygen. Sweat. Hair follicles. Smelly feet. All on edge, ready for war.

The cowboy man made the first move. "We don't appreciate a ruckus in our establishment." He flared his nostrils like a hippo and stamped his boots. I wanted to ask if they were from the snakeskin leather trailer trash collection, but I let it be.

That would have been too easy.

I did three neck circles and the Olympia wannabes took a half step back. "I've been duped," I said. "The fair lady isn't from Athens, Greece. She's from Georgia."

Magrece crinkled her nose and gathered her toys. In the few seconds it took to bring the cavalry, she'd managed to put her robe and panties back on. Not that the cowboy man cared. He'd seen it all.

"Mister," the cowboy man said, "this can go one of two ways. You let these fine gentlemen escort you off the premises. You will not be charged for wasting my girl's time. But we'll take your picture and you won't be allowed back here ever again. Or you can play champ and you won't make it to your fight tomorrow."

Options were sublime.

I said, "Taking a photograph without consent is a violation of the eavesdropping act."

The cowboy man snorted. "As you wish, sir."

He nodded to his cronies and the fun began.

Just bring it.

Pride cometh before the fall. In every conflict, the weakest link usually takes the first step. A show of force. A false sense of superiority. A punch, kick, swipe, or bite that hit air and made the situation much worse. Air meant failure and failure meant being on the defensive. One less body to deal with.

Crony 1 was the weakest link. He charged first and I connected with a jab and sent him into next week.

Crony 2 used the distraction to charge me from behind, but I've seen much worse. I elbowed him in the solar plexus and a right hook afterward left him counting far too many sheep for this world.

Cronies 3 and 4 cut the semicircle in half and tiptoed slowly my way.

I said, "If Hava Nowa comes in here and throws a punch, that'll be all she wrote."

They looked confused and tried the only tactic they knew. Double trouble. They charged simultaneously, one diving at my chest and the other at my ankles. We weren't on the gridiron and we weren't in a pro wrestling ring. Cronies 3 and 4 would never make the same mistake again.

I got Crony 3 with a right uppercut, and blood poured from his nose. I stepped on Crony 4's wrist and pressed down hard. Gravity is the best bully sometimes.

Magrece screamed, but since she'd already hit the panic button there wasn't anything more she could do but watch the fray unfold. Trouble didn't come in eights.

Cronies 5 and 6 took three steps back. They were the newbies. The future enforcers of Toots Life. But for now they were a bunch of nada. Watch and learn, hombres. I charged at them and they ran away.

That left Crony 7. He got me in the back of the head, and I crumpled to the ground. In every fight, one person has all the balls and game. It wasn't mutually exclusive, but when that same person brought the fight, things got much more interesting. A boring fight wasn't a fight at all.

He kicked me in the back and said, "Get the fuck up."

I reached for his legs, but he kicked me in the back of the head some more. "You're running out of time, champ. Let it go."

He laughed, and it sounded like a pre-pubescent boy laugh. Like he was still coming into his own. Coming to terms with being the king of the new jungle.

Cool.

Gotta dethrone the actual king first.

I shook off the cobwebs, grabbed his right leg, and flipped him onto his back. I threw a hard right that connected with his jaw, and I got back to my feet. Sal wouldn't like my form, but function beat form in a street fight. Cold hard facts.

But Crony 7 hopped back to his feet like a ninja. He threw a flurry of combinations, connecting with every third punch. Maybe he was the king. In every fight the cumulative damage does you in. There comes a time when your brain sings a tune and your legs feel like Jell-O. A fighter never knows when to call it quits. He has a corner for that.

And that's what did me in.

No corner in this place.

I blocked a few more of the guy's punches. Out of the corner of my eye I saw Magrece bawling her eyes out. She knew the score. It didn't take a math aficionado to figure it out. Crony 7 was up, and I was down.

And in the heat of battle, the lines get blurred.

Hubris rules the roost and doth forget the rest.

I got Crony 7 with a left hook, but the cowboy man got me with a body shot from behind. I fell to the ground like Humpty Dumpty off that wall.

The cowboy man said, "And I had my money on you tomorrow night."

He spit on my face and kicked me with the heel of his boot.

And everything went black.

21

I woke up with a seatbelt around my waist and a pair of Ray-Bans over my pupils. My left ear heard a whistling seashore and my right ear heard a symphony. My nose itched like a chinchilla and my back felt like a slab of concrete. Just another day as an amateur sleuth.

"I knew this was a bad idea," Sims said.

He was driving the Escalade this time and I was riding shotgun.

"Agreed," I said. "You don't have the credentials the other chauffeur had. He picked up that cage with three fingers."

"He's a keeper." Sims furrowed his brows and gripped the steering wheel till his knuckles turned white.

"He took the long route to the airport. He should be flogged." I looked out my window at the stars glistening off the metallic hulks on the highway. It was late, but Vegas was the new city that never sleeps.

"You could have got yourself killed," Sims said. "And for what? To get some pussy."

"I had Nowa right where I wanted him. Magrece didn't see

it my way," I said. "And she duped me with Athens, Georgia. Not Greece."

"Hava was doing some Facebook Live shit tonight. You clearly didn't get the memo."

Sims was speaking in code again. I was a growing pup when it came to technology, but still part dinosaur in many respects. Living a Facebook didn't make much sense at all.

I said, "He frequents Toots several times a week."

"Well not fight week, genius. " Sims gripped the steering wheel even tighter and merged onto another strip of highway. With all his excess, he probably hadn't driven a car in years, but if there's a will there's a way. Sims hadn't crashed the car thus far, so all was swell under the circumstances.

"Sal would have a field day in these fine-ass establishments," I said.

"Sal would croak the minute the lineup came out. He almost had a triple bypass last time. Cut the shit. You almost blew your purse twice today."

"The devil's in the details."

"I had to break legs to get them to sign the NDAs. And the cherry on top." He pointed to my sunglasses.

"Cowboy man is one tough sonofabitch. Snakeskin leather." I smiled.

Sims frowned. "You broke six noses and one wrist. Seven bases of liability. Eight if you include the partial jaw impingement to cowboy man. Not so tough."

"Put it on my tab," I said.

"You better believe it. The NDAs don't come cheap." He smiled that weaselly agent-gonna-take-advantage of you smile, and I returned it.

"Great work, Simba."

"Tell Sal to cut the Simba shit."

I laughed, then I got serious.

"Tell HBO I'm not fighting if they don't cover the cost of these miscellaneous expenses."

It was in moments like these that the true sibling rivalry showed. We were siblings by proxy, but even siblings by proxy wanted to beat the shit out of each other sometimes. Sims stared me down, then went back to the road. Then I stared him down, and my eyes went to the road. It went like that for twelve seconds, back and forth like a yo-yo. Then Sims caved. He always did.

"After tomorrow you're taking time off," he said. "You're a loose cannon with all the moolah on the line."

I smiled. "Anything for you, sugar."

Sims said nothing.

So I repeated it for effect.

Then Sims said, "Fine. HBO's gonna cover your latest escapade. No more shit. I'm serious."

I blew Sims a kiss and all was well in Hollywood. Then I looked out the window and noticed the full moon. No bueno. I'd been through mucho tonight already, but a full moon was the icing on top. I braced for more shit till I hit the sack.

"Leroy's still in a coma," Sims said. "But the docs say he'll pull through."

"Great. And the pigs?"

"All's quiet. Still chasing down leads. They'll be chasing them down till your next fight out here."

"If they don't look at Juko's camp, I'm calling a press conference."

"No you're not. Shut the fuck up and keep your head in the game."

"Yes, sir." I smiled and saw Mimi's lips on mine. Then I shook the cobwebs off and saw Sims's oily nose. Damn.

Sims got into the fast lane and flew past a station wagon. "This isn't a damned carpool lane," he muttered.

"Easy, Andretti."

Sims picked up even more speed.

Then I said, "And how did my fur baby take the news of my escapades?"

"He shit all over the patio, and when the maid cleaned it up he shit again in the same spot. Obedience classes, my ass. Whoever gave him that certificate needs fraud charges. How many do-overs did he get?"

"Henri's a gentle soul, but a curious one. He wanted to master the curriculum in chunks."

"Get the curious one back to class or he's not joining the show next time around. Your little girlfriend can take care of him."

"We're one-hundred-percent platonic."

Sims rolled his eyes and took an exit. At the bottom of the ramp he hung a left and a block down we reached our destination. We hadn't spoken about it, but sometimes actions speak louder than words.

I was hungry.

And Sims was hungry.

And it was late.

Sal was a stickler for raw eggs and venison and shakes a la mode in the prep for the fight. But I was all about the cheat foods and Sims did nothing to stop it. He knew my palate better than he knew his own calendar. It'd worked for years, and if it ain't broke don't fix it.

We stopped at In-N-Out. The drive-thru spanned the whole parking lot like an anaconda. It was prime time for the grease aficionados of the world. The inside wasn't any better, so we waited in the Escalade.

I rubbed the top of my head and felt a rough scab by my cowlick. I didn't feel any blood so I couldn't blame the cowboy man for my troubles. I felt around the affected area some more and winced.

Sims scowled. "They should have roughed your ass up more."

"If Magrece had two panic buttons it would have been easy-peasy. But she's as much a victim as I am."

"Gotta love them Georgia pines. Augusta is majestic."

I grinned. "I'll be a member there before you."

Sims told me to go fuck myself, and we inched up in line. We were moving at a snail's pace —half an inch every five minutes. A million more inches and we'd reach the finish line. Slow and steady wins the race. Grease be damned.

I watched three rocker girls sharing a joint at one of the picnic tables with the red-and-white umbrellas.

"Don't even think about it," Sims said.

"They have eccentric art," I said. "I wanna ask them the best spot in town."

"Beat Juko and get a whole sleeve. Hell, I'll book you on Best Ink."

"I gave up my thespian ways," I said. I was bullshitting. I snagged the cop role before my fall and was a beloved detective to millions of people around the world. But acting is acting and breaking skulls is breaking skulls. If I could do both with maximum intensity then you bet your ass Sims would book me. But time and effort are limited.

Breaking skulls has a special place in my heart.

Sims frowned, and the line opened up. The cars in front had their orders taken in a heartbeat, and we were next. So much for the snail.

"Hamburger combo, no pickles, and a vanilla milkshake," Sims said. The order receiver jotted everything down on her notepad.

Sims looked at me, and I had no shame. "Double double,

animal style. A piece of chocolate cake. Fries. Diet Coke. And—"

"And that'll be all," Sims said. He gave the girl his card and we inched closer to our greasy bliss. "That cake is mine, too. I gave you some rope, but Juko's not fucking around tonight."

"Carbs fuel muscle contractions," I said.

Twenty-three seconds later we got our food. Sims didn't like eating and driving and talking so we scarfed everything down right in the parking lot. The rocker girls were still toying with their joint, the anaconda grew again, and the chocolate cake was calling my name.

But it was calling Sims's too.

I really wanted it for extra bulk.

Sims wanted it because I wanted it.

The stare-down didn't last long.

Mimi called and everything changed.

22

Mimi said, "Your court days are far from over."

I said, "Thanks for the positivity."

Sims wiped some ketchup off his lower lip and got back on the road. He tossed the napkin out the window like a boss.

"I got summoned back for a reason." Mimi's phone blistered in the background like some kind of bubble wrap.

"I appreciate the smooch," I said.

Mimi said nothing. 'Twas the greatest tool in a woman's arsenal. One minute you're riding high thinking of the moon and the stars and all that sentimental shit, and the next minute you're in the dog house. The experts never told a man when to break the silence or how to break it or when. The male species was supposed to interpret from all the surrounding facts and circumstances. Go for it too early and you were a goner. Go for it too late and the silent treatment persisted.

But find the right moment and you were in the upper echelon of super cool hombres.

I bided my time while Sims reached into his cup holder and

took a swig from a metal water bottle. He was a conundrum. He disregarded the environment with his napkin tosses then in the same breath saved the environment with his reusable canister. The water bottle said "Take No Prisoners" on it and I wanted to toss it out the window for lack of originality. Sims gave me a look that said *who in the blue hell is on the phone* and I gave him a look that said *my girl*. Then Sims smiled and changed lanes like a madman.

The silent treatment persisted for seventeen seconds, and right when I was about to speak up, Mimi said, "How soon can you get to Portland?"

"After my fight, I'm all yours, missy."

More silence on the other end of the line. Then: "You have to be here tomorrow."

"Things are moving too fast for my taste." I said it the way a comedian says it. Short. Punchy. Bullshitty. I was teasing, of course. But that's another thing they don't teach you in the seduction game. When to directly state your intentions and when to tiptoe around them like a ballerina at the Joffrey Ballet. I leaned toward the ballet side of things constantly. The female sex was an enigma to me, but I was an even bigger enigma to them. By design.

"Listen, they made a mistake," Mimi said.

"Oxytocin is the best medicine sometimes."

"You're a person of interest."

"Say it like you mean it, baby."

Sims grinned and picked up speed. He'd been party to many of my salacious conversations over the years. He never butted in, but he always listened and gave hilarious commentary afterwards. He'd lined his pockets off my life, and there wasn't a chance in hell he'd play softie now. And as an added bonus, since he was on payroll, I didn't need an NDA.

"Shut up," Mimi said.

"I can't help it. Too many concussions."

"Wow."

"At some point they stop hibernating and say hello."

"You're a person of interest," Mimi repeated.

"Thanks," I said.

"No. I mean it. You're being subpoenaed for tomorrow."

There comes a point in every conversation with a suit where the class difference comes out front and center. Before that any person could smile and nod and ask questions and give answers. But when the rubber hit the road, the suits stole the show and the rest of us bit the dust and hung on for dear life. We needed the finest dictionaries and the finest mental acuity to grasp all the fine details. We needed an education.

I was no slouch when it came to legal lingo. I got my law degree from the University of Hard Knocks with a certificate in making hooch and shanks on the inside. I had all the right *pro se* motions and tips and tricks.

Yet Mimi flummoxed me this time.

"A quorum of grand jurors is investigating the attempted murder of Maximo Bentini," she said. "Sixteen strong. They're halfway through their eighteen-month term. Now they have this doozy to investigate. Normally it's a nine-to-five kinda thing. Work hard during the week and kick back on the weekends. But now they're working this one up on a Saturday. They have subpoena power and they can summon whoever the hell they want to question them. They can take their sweet ole time and nobody in the defense bar can do anything about it. They're secret proceedings and all lawyers for the witnesses have to stay outside during questioning."

"Doesn't sound so secret," I said.

"It's amazing what old clients can do when you've saved them from the feds."

"The grand jury can indict a ham sandwich. What the hell do they need me for? Right before I kick Juko's ass."

More silence.

Here we go again. The legal morass. The lack-of-criminal-justice system. The wrinkly suits and the dirty robes. The grand jurors called all the shots. They had months to conclude their investigation and vote on whether or not to charge the accused. In legalese it was called a true bill of indictment. Which didn't quite concern me in the grand scheme of things because I was a witness, not a defendant. But something didn't sit right. It smelled rotten to the damned core. They were dropping the hammer as painfully as possible. Whoever loved fucking with me could have just as easily tossed me in jail for the weekend on some bogus charges. Instead, I was being called in as a witness to waste my damned time on the stand till migraine became my middle name again.

And my fight fell away like a couple of old graham crackers.

"Work some lawyer magic and make it go away," I said.

"If I could, I would. But it's a federal investigation. Big leagues."

"Great."

"Since it's federal, the subpoena is enforceable across state lines."

"Thanks for the heads-up. I'm not going to jail."

Those were the magic words Sims needed to hear. He grabbed the phone with his right hand while holding the wheel in a vise grip with his left. For a second I thought he was gonna throw my poor Jitterbug right onto the beltway and make me a full dinosaur again. I had all my contacts in there.

But then he put the phone on speaker.

"You're the cutest jailhouse lawyer I know," Mimi said.

"Cut the shit. He's not going around any courts and any

jails before his fight. You can book that." Sims had steam coming out of his ears.

More silence. Mimi had had a reasonable expectation of privacy on the other end of the line and Sims had ruined the party.

No bueno.

"Are you back at the bachelor pad yet?" she asked.

Sims said, "It's a training ground. But no."

"The feds don't play. The minute you show up you're gonna get served. No ducking it."

I cut in. "Two right hooks and they go to sleep."

Sims merged onto another strip of highway and the wheel was gasping for a second chance at life.

"I'm gonna plead the fifth," I said.

"No," Sims said. "You didn't do anything wrong."

"I saw nada. I did nada. Why give the assholes the satisfaction?"

"You plead the fifth, they'll get a true bill the minute you leave the stand," Mimi said. "Portlandians don't do well with secrets. Then they'll want you as a conspirator." She laughed and I wanted her next to me. It'd been over seven hours since we'd ditched the word *platonic*. If I could reach through the phone and pull her back to Vegas I would.

"They can't investigate shit without an accused," Sims said. "Who's the defendant here—or did that part slip your mind?"

"Excuse me?" Mimi said.

"You heard me."

I smacked Sims on the crown of his head and the Escalade veered slightly onto the shoulder. Sims shook off the cobwebs and then apologized to Mimi.

Mimi said some passerby was accused, but they were grasping at straws to placate the community.

Then the Escalade took an exit ramp and retraced all the

steps back to the rental house. The city was popping at night, but the burbs were all tranquility. I lowered my window and took in the stillness. That's what had drawn Sims to the place from the get-go, but all good things come to an end sometime.

When we pulled up to the house, a gray Crown Vic took up half the driveway. It was parked at a weird angle and had dusty windows from the Sahara.

It took me a few seconds to realize that nobody was in the car.

The feds were banking on the confusion.

When my eyes went back to the inside of the Escalade, I got served.

23

Sims spewed every legal technicality in the book, but the feds puffed their chests out and walked all over him. Shiny badges and fancy guns had something to do with it, but when you got down to brass tacks the feds were calm, collected, and just plain cool. The combo was muy bueno. For them, but not for me.

I stared at the piece of paper in my hands and marveled at the power of it. 'Twas nothing more than an 8.5-by-11-inch glossy paper with some bold Times New Roman font and some fancy Latin terminology. *Subpoena ad Testificandum. You are summoned to testify before the grand jury regarding an incident that occurred on or about...* Yeah, yeah, yeah. I knew the words better than the back of my hand. Legal jargon copied and pasted from the government machine. From the hard drive of a shitty laptop some poor schmuck front-line prosecutor owned to some ramen-noodle intern's printer to some donut desk sergeant working third watch to the assholes who served me with it. Efficiency at its finest in the lack-of-criminal-justice system.

The feds hightailed it out of Dodge, leaving me and Sims behind. The maid came out on the front steps with Henri. The maid shouted in Spanish, but Henri had other plans. He bounded off the front steps and almost bowled over Sims on his way to licking my face off. The poor guy had been cooped up all day inside while I played sleuth. I rubbed Henri's belly, ears, and nose. Then I apologized for all the neglect, and Henri was cool. He rushed back inside while the maid gave chase. Muddy paws in a big rental were not a good combo.

"Call the fight," I said.

"Hell no." Sims rubbed his temples, and I was sure his lawyerly brain was working a million miles per hour. It was times like these where I had the feeling that Sims wished he could trade it all in and haggle in court again. It gave him a rush, and made him king of the hill. I'd never seen Sims in court, but I'd heard stories of him eviscerating people on cross. The more witnesses cried, the more Sims twisted the knife.

"By the time I get back, it's fight time," I said.

Sims was ready. "No. We stick to a strict schedule. The jet'll be waiting at Troutdale. In and out. Hit the stand. Don't volunteer shit you don't have to. Run your mouth for a couple hours, fly back. No detours. No funny business. You're back by five. Fight's around midnight, champ."

Sims had all the answers. That's what he told himself anyway. But the fight game is more than just the fight. It's all about the mental warfare. I wondered if my mind would be right. One minute I'd be arguing with judges and lawyers again, and the next I'd be dodging punches from the number one contender in the world. The average human brain could compartmentalize only so many tasks. The name of the game was to prioritize all the important ones. Use mnemonics. Figure the shit out. It was a trillion-dollar business for the forgetful. Add in fried brain cells, and memory games became far more suspect. Sims wanted my mind on the fight, but my mind was on the courtroom. When you're read your last rites and hoisted on a gurney seconds away from your demise, something's gotta give. But the law stuck to me like Gorilla Glue. I knew that whatever I did in this new world, dammit, Lady Justice would rear her ugly talons and never let me go.

And then there was Mimi.

The star of my eye. The best public defender I had the pleasure of knowing. Damned right I had my mind on the courtroom. One day ago we were complete strangers. Then came furry play dates and platonic kisses in the backseat of a nice Escalade. Mimi knew the score, and she'd tipped me off before it all went to shit. She was a keeper in a world of non-keepers and non-starters.

I looked at Sims like he had the plague. "Benjamins don't cure your heart."

"Cry me a river."

My poignant moment dissipated faster than you can say hombre.

We went inside, and Sims worked his phone so fast I thought he'd bust the circuitry of all the fruit phones in all mankind. He smiled and barked orders and took confirmation numbers and made quid pro quos to his Rolodex of contacts. Twelve minutes later he was all done, and so was Henri. He'd fallen asleep at the foot of the couch.

Sims said, "The Nevada Athletic Commission got the heads-up. They're not leveling any suspensions or canceling the bout on account of pending legal matters that you aren't the subject of."

"Not till the sharks tip their hand," I said. "They have better counselors."

Sims forced a smile. He knew the way things went down on these things, but he didn't feel the effects the way I did. While

Sims fielded scripted questions in every interview in every time zone, I had no script—and even if I did, the sharks were always determined to go off-script anyway. If they had their way, they'd cancel the fight and Juko's bogus smile would carry the cycle. Since he technically would have never lost, he'd have an argument that he deserved the title shot next. The sharks would feed the machine and the crowd would clamor for more.

But Sims wasn't in my league. Plain and simple.

My title.

That I never lost.

Not happening, hombre.

I told Sims to release an official statement. I started by giving him my oral statement, and he texted it to Mandy. She would go into overdrive and spin the words with the best of them.

Then Sims's phone chimed like all the fruit phones.

"Channel 7," Sims said.

He grabbed a remote and turned on the flat-screen TV. He found Channel 7 a few seconds later, and lo and behold, my face was front and center once again. Damn, I was good at that. My pearly whites were, too. I had an awesome smile. The news anchor talked about the fight and my legal troubles, then they cut to a man in orange spectacles live on location in Portland. He talked about my legal history and the alleged facts of this new case. I was referred to as a "recidivist" a couple times before they went back to studio. They got everything wrong, but they weren't being paid for veracity. Ratings equaled power. Conspirators had cachet.

But Mandy had more.

One of the anchors tapped her ear and looked confused. Then she said, "We have an official statement from the Lance Gedrin team." She read the statement, and the cameraman plastered it all over the screen for two minutes. It was long and comical and ridiculous and pointed. It hit all the right points at all the right times. If I had to estimate, three percent of it had to do with actual fighting, while the rest of it had to do with perseverance and flying in the face of rumor and false advertising. A good percentage of it was bullshit. But selling is selling.

I got my point across.

The anchors debated my statement for a few seconds then cut to a story on an armed robbery in suburbia.

"You're a natural," Sims said.

"I learned from the best."

"Sounds about right." Sims looked at his phone, and when it didn't ring on his command he seemed flustered.

I put a hand on his shoulder. "When I get to the top of that mountain, I might trade in the gloves for some nice Italian suits."

"I'm gonna die young."

"Shut the fuck up. I wanna fight for the wrongfully convicted."

"You've given me enough heart attacks since you got out. Let's table this discussion."

"This ain't easy work." I smiled, and Sims returned it. We looked out at the patio and the stars that peeked through the partially drawn shades. I would have held my gaze there for a long time, but my body was on autopilot.

Big day tomorrow.

I crashed on the couch and got some of the best shuteye I'd had in a very long time.

24

I woke up in the same plush king bed as the day before. The keen observer would say I was an unreliable narrator or that this was a sleight of hand, a deception of epic proportions. But it was neither. I was a sleepwalker. It started after I got out of the joint and would rear its hideous head every third day. I didn't know what the significance of the third day was, but assimilation is the name of the game. Adapt or perish. When I woke up in a different stead from my previous nights I realized that others had it far worse. A few geriatric cons waxed poetic on the inside about stabbings and hijackings and a host of other "-ings" that followed the super-serious sleepwalkers.

I was normal.

All day.

I stretched my body out on the bed and did seven snow angels against the Egyptian cotton. I did three neck circles to stretch out all the tissue upstairs, and then I hopped off the bed and pounded out thirty pushups. Getting a pump before the big day was finer than the finest wine in Napa Valley. I hopped back to my feet and saw that my clothes were laid out for me. A hanger with a whole ensemble was stuck to one of the cabinet knobs like bubble gum. I didn't like it one bit. I never asked for help in the clothing department. And I sure as hell didn't need any. I was a fashionista. Plain and simple. The clothes weren't for casual wear, but I described fabrics the way a scientist described string theory. With the utmost care and precision.

But court was a whole other animal. Court clothes told a story and could very well make the judge your friend or your foe. Every inch would be scrutinized by the sharks. They'd have round table discussions and fashion police segments. I once was all but unrecognizable on the streets. I could eat my pancakes and let the sugary goodness course through my veins while I exhaled deeply and took the next hit. After a few doses of sugary goodness I could untuck my shirt and get second and third helpings. Hell, I could get fifth helpings if I fancied it. But when you're put through the wringer by an overzealous prosecution twice, anonymity goes out the window.

Shame.

Pancakes were to be worshipped in peace and with decorum.

Sims had picked out a navy-blue suit, off-white Brooks Brothers dress shirt, dark-brown monk strap dress shoes, light-brown socks that went past the knees, and an orange handkerchief. He must have conspired with a vogue stylist to keep my fashion game on point. The handkerchief was damned good, but one thing was missing from the equation.

Cufflinks.

They made the whole piece.

Button cuffs screamed amateur. No cuffs screamed the sloppiest of slobs. The wrong cuffs—well, that was almost worse than murder in a fashion blogger's eyes. Sims didn't pick up on these finer details. That was what separated the wheat from the chaff. The big boys from the pretenders.

I knew just the trick.

Before I could work my magic, Sims walked into my room.

"Showtime, champ. PJ's back by three. In and out like we said. Food's on the counter. Dry. No sauces."

I said, "Swell. And a bucket of cufflinks."

Sims shook his head, and then it dawned on him. He explained his error in full, but I ignored him entirely.

Sims walked over to the window, parted the blinds a quarter-inch, and peered through the crevice like he was hiding a national security asset.

"Get ready for your strut," he said.

"You mean my perp walk?"

"It's not a perp walk. You didn't do anything wrong."

"Semantics. The bag man walks out and his irises get bombarded with the worst possible light."

"You want a medal? No shenanigans today."

I smiled. "Yes, padre. But one thing."

I repeated my gripe about the cufflinks and Sims looked like he was going to have a heart attack. Then he left, and I heard him traipsing around his big-boy rental searching and then asking the maid for direction. I thought it was a fruitless endeavor. Cufflinks were always well-camouflaged in plush locales. I'd just have to be the schmuck without cufflinks in front of the grand jury.

But seven minutes later, Sims came through. He returned with sweat beads dotting his forehead, but when he held out his hand it held two of the best damned cufflinks I'd ever seen. Orange hue with diamond engravings.

Sims smiled. "Shysters always get the job done."

"The orange hue matches the handkerchief," I said. "It's all about fluidity and making a good impression. You've absorbed a lot over the years." I raised my eyebrows to accentuate the point.

Sims flicked me off.

I put on the orange cufflinks and looked at myself in the mirror. A hunk looking like a baller before the big game. The judge wasn't going to do shit when he saw me. I owned the place.

I went downstairs. Henri must have realized it was a big day because instead of jumping on me and soiling my awesome attire he just sniffed my hand and turned his attention to his water bowl. I downed a fruity omelet and went back upstairs to brush my teeth, then came back down and Henri was gone. I searched all over for him, then realized he was on the patio taking a nap.

The perro life.

When I turned around, a driver stood in the doorway.

"Mr. Gedrin," he said, "my team is positioned on the perimeter. Don't pause for any autographs. We haven't secured the whole area. It's a moving situation."

"What about the sharks?" I asked.

"What, sir?"

"The cameras?"

The driver shook his head. "Any time you stop it's a threat. I've had clients get their heads blown off for not listening. Those cameras don't exist."

"Can't hit what you can't see, man." I shadowboxed the driver for a few seconds. He wasn't amused.

Then Sims came downstairs, shook the driver's hand and told him to wait outside.

I looked over at Sims. "Team militia now?"

"That's Marko. The best of the best. Did two tours in Iraq then set up shop in the Palisades. The driving is a bonus. I'm not taking any chances after all this shit." He put his hand on my shoulder. "Good luck, grasshopper."

"Keep an eye on Sal."

"He's got his own detail. Marko made sure of it."

"He better, or the best security team in the world can't hold me back. I'll lay the smackdown on all their candy asses."

Sims pushed me out the door, and the minute I walked out the sharks hit me with their best shot. My irises were ready though. They shouted and pushed and prodded, but I stayed cool. Marko guided me into the backseat of the Escalade, and that's all she wrote.

We hightailed it to a private airstrip where Sims's jet was waiting. It was a different one from Portland. I walked up the steps, and a few minutes later we were airborne.

A solid operation by a solid hombre. I never saw Marko again.

But I should have had him on speed dial.

25

Seventy minutes later I was standing in front of the Mark O. Hatfield Courthouse in downtown Portland. The gray facade stretched into the sky like Gumby as sheriffs' deputies milled around all points of ingress and egress. My middle name might as well have been the law because I was mixed up in it more than a matador in the ring with all the bulls. It stuck to me like the finest glue.

On a Monday the place would be teeming with fuckups trying to get their due in the hallowed halls of justice. They'd line the security entrances and complain about the judge and the clerk and their counselor. Their arguments would fall flat because unlike the typical state courtrooms, federal court was the big leagues. A cut of cloth far above the rest. You felt it the moment you walked into the joint. From the marble hallways to the plaques and inscriptions on the walls to the leather seating and ambient lighting, the feds played nice. In the ambiance department at least. As well as I knew the court system's quirks, I'd never been in federal court before.

I was a fed virgin.

But today was Saturday, and there were no lines. Score one point for me. And the special grand jury session hadn't brought out the sharks, apparently. I walked in the front entrance and went through security in thirty seconds. Two of the deputies had confused looks on their faces that said, *Don't I know that guy?* And I had a confused look on my face that said, *Aren't there any cup holders for phones here?*

I trudged on and followed the sparse foot traffic. Which was hopeless because for every person taking a right and a left, there was a straggler taking two lefts and then a right. The signage didn't help the cause either, so I went with team straggler. I took two lefts and then a right. Then I found a bank of escalators and took them up.

Bingo.

I saw a sign for the grand jury room and followed. But then I came across a big red sign that read: *STOP. Grand Jury in Progress.* The entrance was roped off like the red carpet was about to be rolled out at the Oscars.

I stood there and waited. I was subpoenaed, which meant that I was at the whim of the prosecutor. Sims wanted me back by three, but what if the assholes didn't call me as a witness until three? The slick prosecutor would flash his yellow canines and belabor the point till the cows came home. And just when you'd think he was all done, he'd add some more hundred-dollar words on top of it all.

But truth be told, the grand jurors called the shots. They indicted the ham sandwiches, so they could get me outta here quick. One look at my worthless testimony and they'd send me on my way faster than I could say hola. As I pondered the nuances, I heard a familiar voice.

"You clean up nice."

I turned, and there was Mimi. She wore Gucci glasses, her curls were tucked into a ponytail, and her body was in a tight beige suit that screamed badass boss girl. If I cleaned up nice, Mimi cleaned up *hella* nice.

I gave her one of my wider smiles, and Mimi grinned back. We stood there for a few seconds like a couple of school kids returning from summer break. There was so much to say, yet I froze. Nothing came out. Maybe Mimi had the same issue, because I could see the gears churning in her head, but nothing came from her lips either. The meetup right after a first kiss can either set the stage for things to come or be the harbinger of death. Ah, the beauty of courtship.

The stage was certainly set.

Finally, Mimi said, "You've got this."

"Thanks, counselor. You public servants have all the right syllables."

Mimi laughed, and my chest fluttered and asked for more. I was semi-asthmatic.

"Where's Henri?" Mimi asked.

"As much as I would love Henri to meet Judge Asshole, I think he's better suited to large patios and Sin City."

"The rascal. Just like his daddy."

Mimi fixed my tie and patted the shoulder pads of my jacket. Women were great with the micro-details, and men were great at thinking they were great with the micro-details.

I looked Mimi up and down and grinned. "Where's Bruce to escort you around these hallowed halls? How you gonna sit with those spinal issues?"

"Bruce is a little under the weather. Too many treats on the plane ride over. He doesn't process chicken byproducts all that well. And he's not a fan of tranquilizers either. But the king will live. I can't go inside anyway."

I forgot that this wasn't a regular court appearance. 'Twas a secret, and that extended to lawyers for all the witnesses. Mimi couldn't be my lawyer anyway because she represented the fine indigent clients of Portland accused of state offenses both big and small. But even if she decided to hang a shingle in that moment she couldn't. Secrecy was the name of the game. The grand jurors were stealthy arbiters of justice.

"I should have stayed with the monkeys," I said.

"Everything happens for a reason."

Mimi let the words hang. Those micro-details again. I could make inferences, but never the right ones. Accuracy eluded me like it eluded the Bears quarterbacks on Sundays. Was Mimi saying that fate brought us together, or was she saying that I had some greater purpose? Perhaps to take the fall again for a bullshit crime I didn't do.

As I stood there, rubbing my forehead, Mimi took out her phone and started texting. She was good with the keys, but then she put the phone back in her pocket quicker than you could say bueno.

"What's your favorite fruit?" I said.

Mimi looked confused. Then I said fruit again and did air quotes. She was still confused.

"Your phone. What kinda fruit," I said.

Mimi laughed. "It's an iPhone, Grandpa. Get with the program."

"Technology is the bane of my existence sometimes. Teach me the ways, missy."

She grinned. "That won't be a problem at all."

She moved a little closer to me. We were the only people in the hallway and the only sound was the hum of the central air. For a moment I thought I heard sheriff walkies around the corner, but then it went away. It was probably security for the back entrance of the courtroom.

In life there are winners and there are losers. The losers usually play it safe and don't have the balls to go all out. Some would say it's in their DNA to quit. They fold faster than a bad round of dominoes. They play Jenga and they're shouting it from the rooftops.

But the winners get it.

They have all the skills and all charisma and they can read the room.

I was a winner.

Always.

I took Mimi's hand, and I could feel her breathing getting heavier.

"Cool," I said. "Love at first grand jury."

I pulled her close and kissed her. She kissed back. We took turns till our mandibles got sore. Then we took turns again and again and again. I don't remember how long it was, partly because I wasn't counting and all good things come to an end.

Heels clicked around the corner, and we broke apart.

Mimi grinned and I fixed my wardrobe malfunction.

"I'm pleading the fifth," I said.

"Bummer. I'm not attracted to cowards."

"I can be cowardly on half and pristine on the other half."

"No way, Jose."

She was right. And I knew she was right before I even said anything. I just wanted to see her get all worked up with the technicalities.

Muy caliente.

We spent the next few minutes talking about miscellaneous things that were of no import to grand juries or fights or the human condition. At one point I steered the conversation toward pancakes, but then Mimi steered the conversation toward the artwork in her place. I told her I enjoyed critiquing art and that it put me at ease. One look at a piece and I could give a diatribe like a general.

"Say your piece and then you're coming over to tell me how my art really is," she said.

"I gotta be back by three."

I told her all about Sims's plan.

"Everybody needs some inspiration," she said.

I'd make it back by three all right.

Then the heels returned. This time they got louder and rounded the corner. And just like that the vibe was ruined for me and for Mimi. Life's a riot sometimes.

It was Detective Finley. He parted the rope blocking off the courtroom, looked back at me and said, "Isn't it fight night? Things about to get lit, champ."

He smiled and walked into the courtroom.

26

Sixteen minutes later a deputy came out. I was summoned. I squeezed Mimi's hand and scurried around the velvet rope. I pushed the left door and heard the deputy fasten the rope behind me. The metal clip clanged off the pole like a church bell in a small village. The deputy gave me directions, but I wasn't paying attention. I wanted to find Finley. But he was gone. As I walked down the middle of the courtroom I wondered who'd ferried him away through the secret entrance. Courthouses were known for shit like that. Little side doors where judges, lawyers, cops, and even custody dudes could make a break for it. Finley had all the connects. He'd spewed his bullshit and was given the VIP treatment and ducked out. Now he was back roaming the streets giving hell to the rest of the Oregonians.

I passed through a small wooden gate that was more decoration than impediment. The jury box lined the left side of the room. There were twenty jurors in total, all staring at me like I had the plague. Some long mahogany tables were to my right, and they took the cake as far as decor was concerned. Lawyerly tomes stood upright and crinkly legal pads were tossed askew next to them. One fat suit sat in a plush leather chair and motioned me toward the witness stand.

And of course, how could I forget about the man of the hour? The judge sat atop his throne with the ugliest green spectacles I'd ever seen. I couldn't make out his nameplate and after a lifetime in the courts it didn't matter. Another day in the system. Another day going up against the man. Another day hearing legal diarrhea back and forth. 'Twas the way of the world. I was sworn in by the judge and took my seat.

My body language said I was comfortable and I'd been here before. But the view was unfamiliar. No one in the gallery. No prying eyes. No muted whispers and snickers. No grins. Secret really meant secret. The grand jurors didn't fool around.

Judge What's-His-Face said, "Mr. Gleason, your witness."

The suit at the table stood up and buttoned the first button of his suit jacket. His white Oxford dress shirt poked out and wouldn't stay put. I guessed this fat hombre was Mr. Gleason. After a while they all looked, smiled, and acted the exact same way in the machine. Which is to say clueless and entitled and an asshole.

Gleason walked to a lectern, opened a binder, and arranged some pages. "State your name for the grand jurors, please."

"Lance Gedrin."

"Mr. Gedrin thank you for coming in on such short—"

"My pleasure."

"Let him finish the question," the judge said.

"I heard a compliment, not a question, Your Honor."

I glanced over at the grand jurors. Several of them were amused. But several of them were not. The latter were more amused with their fruit phones. I wanted to tell them pears were the best, but that would have been too easy.

The judge gave me the death stare, and I nodded my apologies.

Gleason continued. "Thanks for coming in on such short notice, Mr. Gedrin. I know this isn't easy for you to talk about with these fine citizens of Portland, Oregon, but civic duty is civic duty. Let's get to the bottom of this and you can tell us your story."

"No problemo."

The judge shot me a look, and this time several more grand jurors were amused. I was making real progress.

If Gleason was amused, he didn't show it. He went back to his binder and flipped through some of the pages. He did that for twenty seconds before his eyes locked in on mine.

"Let me direct your attention to July ninth at ten a.m. A couple days ago. Where were you?"

"The Oregon Zoo."

"Please tell the ladies and gentlemen of the grand jury what you were doing there."

"Playing with the monkeys."

Three-fourths of the grand jurors almost keeled over laughing.

The judge's face was red.

Gleason hadn't expected my answer. "What?" he said.

"Henri was playing with the monkeys and I watched."

I figured that if there was any possibility of getting railroaded in this proceeding, and there always was, I might as well go out with grand ceremony. I'd be cracking jokes all the way to the pen to preserve my sanity.

The judge scowled. "Mr. Gedrin, this isn't a game."

"I took an oath, Your Honor. I was with my dog, Henri. He's a service dog."

"Your service dog Henri was playing with the monkeys?" Gleason asked.

"Yes. He's fascinated by certain mammals, and they hit it off from the start. So I did what any respectable fur parent would do. I let him play with the monkeys. I supervised. He played nice for a while, then things got out of hand. So I called it quits."

Gleason fixed his tie cautiously. "By play, do you mean in the actual monkey enclosure?"

"There was a glass enclosure. Henri stood outside and barked, while the monkeys pressed their faces to the glass and made all those monkey noises. I don't remember which. But I can imitate them if you like."

Four grand jurors grinned, and out of the corner of my eye I saw another four taking notes.

"That won't be necessary," Gleason said. "What happened next?"

"After the playdate had run its course, I moved on to another exhibit."

"And would that be the African painted dog?"

"Yes, counselor. Beat me to it."

"Why did you go there?"

In a normal courtroom and under normal circumstances any defense lawyer worth his or her salt would object on a variety of grounds. Arguing with the witness. Leading. Relevance. To name a few. The real lawyers would find all the technicalities and go to town. But grand juries indict ham sandwiches for a reason. The prosecutors control the narrative and the grand jurors sit there licking their chops. I was a succulent little lamb waiting for the slaughter.

"The zoo is so large," I said. "I can't walk all that with Henri. He gets hangry. So I settled for the best exhibit in the place."

"And how did you determine that?"

"Foot traffic."

Gleason furrowed his brow, and more of the buttons on his shirt peeked out from his suit jacket.

I waved my arms for effect. "Foot traffic means one of two things. Either the exhibit is really great and the masses are following it to get that memory on their phones. Lot of fruit these days. Or it means there's trouble afoot."

Before I could expand on my hypothesis, Gleason said, "And you knew there was trouble afoot, didn't you?"

Three of the grand jurors sat ramrod straight in their seats.

What a shit show.

I shook my head. "Henri's ever the optimist, and that's rubbed off on me too. I thought it'd be a great exhibit. So we went there with haste."

"And when you got to the exhibit, trouble was really afoot, correct?" Gleason fixed his tie, and I wanted to take it and punch it through his mountain of a stomach. The asshole was trying to work the room with that sly grin. And wannabe facial hair.

"I came upon a crowd of people," I said. "And when the crowd parted, trouble would be an understatement."

"What happened next?" Gleason said.

"I pushed through the crowd and found a man lying on the ground."

"What's the man's name?"

"Maximo Bentini."

"And you had a relationship with this man, didn't you?"

"Easy there, counselor. It wasn't like that. But I knew him back in the day."

"Not just back in the day, Mr. Gedrin. I remind you, you're under oath here. The man currently works for you, right?"

"He was my cutman for my fights. And after a long hiatus, he's back as my cutman."

The grand jurors had no idea what the hell a cutman was.

The general public looked down upon the fight game and cast all its participants as villains, no matter the circumstances. Juvenile barbarians who never quit. That was how they saw us. Drugged-up killing machines who didn't deserve to walk the same streets as them. The minute "cutman" came out of my mouth at least ten of the jurors scribbled in their notebooks.

"And why the hiatus, Mr. Gedrin?"

"*Objection!*" I said.

The judge had his mouth open. Gleason too. The grand jurors stopped scribbling. Take that! I'd been in a lot of court-rooms and knew all the tricks. If your opponent is scoring points, you have to score back. *Carpe diem*. Seize the day. Stop the bleeding. Misdirect. Confuse. Grab their attention and never let go.

The judge fixed his spectacles and pointed his finger at me. "Mr. Gedrin, if you have an outburst like that in my courtroom again you will be held in contempt of this court. Witnesses cannot object. That's what the attorneys are for. If this court feels that counsel has made some sort of legal error, then this court will object on its own accord and note it for the record. Understood?"

I played it cool. "Yes, Your Honor. Easy-peasy."

"Good. Now answer the question."

I turned back to Gleason. "I was on hiatus at Pontiac Correctional for a murder I didn't commit. Did twelve years, and I'm still waiting on my check."

The grand jurors were scribbling faster now. So much for honesty.

Gleason went back to his notes. "You stayed with Mr. Bentini when you saw him in that state, didn't you?"

"Yes. Until the EMTs arrived."

"Isn't it true that you and Mr. Bentini had a falling out?"

"When?"

"Prior to yesterday's incident."

I racked my brain. I'd had falling outs with just about every human I'd ever encountered on this planet, so it was hard to figure out where Bentini stood on the food chain. I closed my eyes and counted to twenty-three.

Nada.

"I do not recall," I said.

"Is your memory exhausted?" Mr. Gleason asked.

"Absolutely, positively."

Mr. Gleason approached with a receipt. I didn't need another look because I knew this shit better than my left hand.

The receipt from the racetrack.

The asshole was laying the foundation .

"I'm showing you a receipt from a racetrack dated July tenth. Take a look at it, and when your memory's refreshed, look up."

I glanced at it, then tossed it back on Gleason's pudgy hands.

Gleason said, "You had a date with Mr. Bentini at the racetrack, didn't you?"

"No."

"After this incident you went back to his motel room and were found snooping around there, isn't that right?"

More scribbling from the peanut gallery.

"I wanted answers on who did this."

"You blasted Detective Finley for stopping you after the incident."

"I sure did. I wanted answers, counselor."

Gleason went back to his binder. He was running out of steam, but I knew better than to celebrate too soon. He'd done no real damage, but the ham sandwiches would be confused, and even the worst lawyers could score a knockout with one stray question or meandering answer. I needed to stay centered.

I thought of Mimi.

Gleason said, "Isn't it true that you threatened Detective Finley?"

To the victor go the spoils.

"No way, hombre."

Gleason asked a few more bullshit questions that went nowhere, and a few minutes later I was walking past the decorative gate, down the hall, out the door, past the velvet rope, and into the hallway.

Mimi was gone.

"I did it," a voice said.

I looked to my left. It was the Blazers man from the zoo.

"It was me," he said. "It's always the con."

27

I tossed the punk against the wall and lifted him up by his scrawny neck. I was in the ring and my goal was the same. See target. Kill target. My eyes narrowed and my brows were like chinchillas. If I were wearing contacts in that moment they'd have given me a million floaters. I kicked the Blazers man's left knee and he gargled in pain. His summer gear was gone. No Oden jersey. No cargos. No Airforce Ones. He'd ditched it all for a charcoal suit with a single vent in back and a light-blue handkerchief in his left breast pocket. His hair was well-coiffed and his shoes were Amish leather.

"Who the fuck are you working with?" I said.

Blazers Man gargled some more. I let him. Asphyxiation is a beautiful thing. I counted the seconds in my head. It took just under ten for the average person to lose consciousness when pressure was applied to the carotid artery.

Three.

Five.

Seven.

Nine.

I broke the hold and the Blazers man held his palms out in surrender.

"What the fuck?" he said.

I held his gaze. "Did I stutter?"

"I didn't do shit, man. Why you gotta be like that? I knew you was goofy from the zoo."

"Honesty is the best policy, hombre."

"They caught up with me," the Blazers man said. He straightened his tie and tried to compose himself.

"Who?"

"Who you think? The same bitches as always."

"Finley."

"Yeah. Right after my PO called me about doing a random drop, all was good. I went back home. Fed the pit and that's when shit hit the fan." He shook his head while he talked and made eye contact every fourth syllable. I didn't know if I trusted him yet. I trusted him before, but trust changes like the seasons.

"What do you feed him?" I asked.

"What?"

"The furry monster. What nutrients do you put into his big belly?"

"What the fuck is it to you?"

Blazers Man took a step forward, and for a second I thought he would dare to take another for me prying into his fur parent habits. But he was smart. He didn't want to get his ass kicked again. He stepped back.

And to make things more interesting, I stepped forward.

Then he stepped even further back.

I said, "A man who treats an animal wrongly can't be trusted with the codes."

The Blazers man shook his head. "Blue Buffalo."

"Swell. Finley."

GREG GOUNTANIS

"I'm feeding my pit. Then a knock at the door. And not just any knock. One of those we've-got-a-warrant knocks. *Police! Police! We're gonna ram, all that shit.* I'm not about to get shot, so I open up. Finley and his newbie partner are smiling like they just got some ass."

"Edgar."

"Bumblefuck for all I know." He crinkled his nose and made a shooing motion with his hand as if to say Edgar was on his hit list.

"What did the blokes do next?"

"They a had tape of me right by the African dog. They played it right on my big screen. Assholes didn't even ask or nothing. They popped a stick in and I'm there on screen. Lot of pixels with that shit."

"Doing nothing but enjoying the Oregon Zoo," I said. "Like any other civilian."

"Or engaging in a conspiracy to commit murder. That's the way Finley saw it. I got the hell out, leaving your boy Bentini clutching his stomach. Everybody else stayed. And then it hits me. I didn't just leave. I sprinted out of that bitch."

"You were in shock and it took you time to process. You weren't ducking punches but you might as well have been. Fight or flight. You chose flight."

"You got railroaded in the Prairie State, right?"

"What?"

"The one who took the rap for murder in Chicago. Bogus charges. I almost got killed by a legend. Respect, brotha."

"I get that a lot."

The Blazers man fist-bumped me and there was nothing I could do about it. One minute asphyxiation, the next mutual admiration. Then the Blazers man smiled and it was the first time I'd ever seen him so much as lift his cheekbones. Which was probably for the best because when he flashed his pearly whites, they were anything but. A four-inch gap separated his upper front teeth, and gold fillings said hello on his rear molars.

"Sue their asses," he said.

I said, "Check's been in transit since Katrina." Truth be told I hadn't checked on the check for quite some time, but then again that was Sims's job. Since my former counselor was a deceased murderer. But once I beat the shit out of Juko the spotlight would be back on those who wronged me. Cut that check.

Blazers Man nodded. "Finley pushes me up against a wall, hands to my throat. Not as strong as you, man, but still fierce. I wanted to kick him in the balls, but then my PO would violate me for sure. Finley tells me to think again on what I saw at the time. I told him to look at the tape again, and—"

"He showed you some more Oregon love."

"Yeah. Motherfucker split my lip. Didn't even give me a towel. Then he goes, 'Did you see that asshole Gedrin there?'"

"I'm a D-lister at this point. I'm at the scene. But they've got shit."

"That's what I said. Then the rookie Edgar's talking about motive and opportunity and 'Did you know he beats people's asses for a living? Did you see him by the body? Think clearly or a grand jury will indict your candy ass as an accessory in a heartbeat.'"

I shook my head. The whole thing felt like amateur hour. Finley and Edgar were two stooges with the brain capacity of half of a stooge. They wanted to mix me up in a bullshit case that Bentini wasn't even going to press charges on. But the more I tossed it back and forth in my head, the more questions I had. Finley was calling the shots, but behind every Finley was an even bigger Finley. Who the hell was the powerbroker who wanted me indisposed before my big fight? My money was on the same asshole who was fucking with my seconds. He'd greased some pockets and fed some bullshit line to Gleason that the victim was hell-bent on prosecution, and now he was watching it all unravel, one thread at a time. The grand jury would indict the ham sandwich and all would fall into place.

No bueno.

Blazers Man continued. "And the fucked-up part? I haven't been called to the stand. No subpoena. Nothing."

I fixed him with a hard stare. "And you expect me to believe you voluntarily came to save my ass?"

"Yessir. I was sticking to my guns."

"Greg Oden sucks," I said.

"Fuck you."

"Conley carried him."

Then Blazers Man asked for an autograph and I obliged. And just like that he was gone. I'd never see him again, but sometimes you gotta cherish the small things in life. The average human interactions with thousands of strangers in your lifetime. If you add all the seconds up, it's quite astonishing, and you realize one immutable truth.

Life is random, but life is beautiful.

I heard footsteps coming down the hall. I was hoping for Finley to show himself again so I could give him a piece of my mind, but the person who came around the corner was even better.

It was Mimi, smiling.

"How'd it go in there, handsome?"

"Sublime."

Mimi gave me a kiss. "Go easy on the artwork."

I looked at my watch and smiled. I had plenty of time to check out Mimi's place.

28

Ten minutes later we were in Nob Hill. The government must have paid finely, because Mimi's place was on Eighteenth Avenue—ten-plus stories of an architect's dream. The shapes and hues and corners were exquisite. I couldn't quite place the year, but if I were a betting man I'd say the decor was no more than three years old. A newbie on scene, flanked by a bunch of Victorian-style storefronts. Globs of steel stretched to the clouds like cathedral spires and the hubbub of downtown traffic wouldn't simmer down.

We went through the revolving doors. The security guard smiled at Mimi and rolled his eyes at me as if to say *Who in the blue hell is this fool ruining my chance with this fine lady?* I made a point of running my eyes over Mimi's booty. I could tell the guard wanted to kill me; a woman of Mimi's caliber had men lining up and filling applications. Luckily for her, I wasn't a jealous hombre. And I wasn't needy.

Mimi and I got in the elevator, and she hit the button for the seventh floor.

"I can't wait to massage Bruce's whiskers," I said.

"He's at doggy day care," Mimi said.

"Sacrilege."

"His momma needs some me time."

"Scoliosis is atrocious."

The elevator opened on seven. Purple carpeting ran left and right, and fake art canvases that looked like real art canvases lined the walls. There were only three units on each side, which meant that Mimi's place was even bigger than I thought. And the government paid even better than I thought.

Mimi stopped in front of a door with a thick mat that said *Welcome Kooks*. Before I could add commentary, Mimi said, "My cousin got me the wrong mat last week."

"Uh-huh."

"Really."

"It has a nice ring to it."

Mimi slapped me on the back and never told me what the mat was supposed to say. I was cool.

She opened her door, revealing a place that looked like it came right out of a bougie-ass catalog. Light cream hardwood lined the whole place and big bay windows overlooked the city and the parks. Mimi's kitchen was new deco and her furniture was urban collective.

I was tempted to ask what style the bedroom was, but it was better to go with the flow in these circumstances.

"Drink?" Mimi said.

I shook my head. "Fighting."

"Loser."

"But I'll take a water, madam. Dehydration is the enemy of success."

Mimi opened her fridge and took out a big water pitcher. She poured me half a glass, then put the cup in the dispenser and added two ice cubes.

"You're boring," she said. "But functional. We all need that sometimes."

"My mama always said to never be a discourteous house-guest. Under any circumstances."

Mimi laughed. "Mama knows best. Except for the boxing part. If I saw her I'd give her a piece of my mind for letting you get into such a horrible sport. How many brain cells did she use when she made that decision?"

There comes a point in every conversation where the scales swing in one of two directions. Direction one is camaraderie. Direction two is awkwardness. This interaction was quickly heading in the latter direction. How do you explain to a woman you're interested in that your mama passed without killing the vibe?

I had no idea, so I said nothing.

Luckily, a woman's intuition is golden. Mimi picked up on it. Lawyers always know what's up.

"Sorry about your mom. I shouldn't have said anything."

"That's okay. It's been a while."

Mimi poured herself a glass of red wine. I wasn't an expert, but I dubbed it a pinot noir. That sounded about right and encompassed a big lot in the vino industry. Sal gave me the scoop once, and I made sure to forget it till I needed it.

Mimi showed me her outer patio, which had a big dirt bike parked in the corner. I asked her all about the gears for several minutes, then she got tired answering the same question nine different ways, and we came back inside.

"Are you nervous about tonight?" she said.

"I've got nerves of steel."

"Bullshit. You're scared of pissing yourself. You're scared one shot could put you in a wheelchair for good. You can liter-ally die in there."

"Thanks for the confidence, missy. We all die, so I'm not keeping tabs on it."

"What's it like to hear somebody's skull break?"

"It's such a horrible sport."

"Stop."

Mimi moved closer, and we were touching shoulder blades now.

"To be honest, it has its perks," I said. Mimi gave me a look, and I gave her a look. The fight game was muy bueno, but I wasn't about to wax poetic about it unless I got more signals.

She showed me to the couch, and we sat down. Me on one end, her on the other. Her right leg took up the middle cushion and she angled it my way. Intimacy grows at a glacial pace until the avalanche comes and there's nothing you can do about it.

My signal.

"The fact that you enjoy dismantling the human body is troubling," Mimi said. "But overall it's kinda hot." She smiled.

I said, "You don't feel it at first. When the glove hits the orbital bone. Then it's like an aftershock. Like bumper cars. You pull back the glove to play defense, but the crunch is unmistakable. The eyes roll back in the head. The guy staggers back half an inch. He wants to throw a counter and get back in the game, but he can't. His legs are Jell-O. He's more fucked than a con at that point."

Mimi kicked me.

I let her.

"You're really something," she said. "A big star who acts like he's on welfare. Not that those on welfare don't have redeemable qualities, but you get my point. You play real safe. I expected more of a bad boy."

"My mansion soirees left a bad taste," I said.

"Your cheap ass never had any mansions. Who are you trying to fool?"

"The pretty girl with the pinot noir."

"It's a cab."

"Cool."

My phone rang. Sims. I knew what he wanted, and I knew what *I* wanted. I let it go to voicemail.

"The pilot is so persistent," I said.

"Curiosity killed the cat."

We locked eyes in that moment, and it was like we'd known each other forever. Some called it the triangular gaze, taking your pupils and going to her pupils, then her mouth, then repeating the triangle. Others called it a damned good moment that changed everything between man and woman. If only for a few seconds.

Our lips said hello again.

Mimi's first.

Then mine.

We took turns but didn't keep score.

Mimi wanted more, and it showed. She moved her body onto the middle seat cushion and ran her finger up my leg to my chest. She pulled me close and kissed me hard. I didn't complain. She did it twice before I joined the party. I ran my hands down the small of her back and kissed her neck twice as hard. She whispered things that I didn't understand and I whispered things that she didn't understand. We took our clothes off and whispered some more.

"You won't hurt me," Mimi said. It was supposed to be a question, but it came out as a statement.

"Not in a million years," I said.

Mimi took my hand and led me to the bedroom. We passed a guest bedroom that had a traditional style and our feet met a fine Persian rug as we moved down the hall. At first the master bedroom threw me for a loop, but then I got used to it.

Scandinavian design.

One of the best living arrangements I'd ever seen.

I didn't do any more analyzing after that.

We fucked.

Again and again and again and again and again.

A fighter isn't supposed to do it before fight night. So sayeth Sal and other old-timers. It purportedly messes with the reflexes.

I strongly disagreed.

Mimi did too.

She taught me a lot of things that afternoon. When it was all over, we were like two crumbled, saltless pretzels on the bed. We smiled and whispered sweet nothings and made plans for events far in the future we knew we couldn't keep.

And the afternoon would have kept going like that, but there was a knock at the door.

Mimi put her clothes on and went to check it out. She wasn't expecting company.

And she certainly wasn't expecting what happened next.

29

Mimi screamed as the door blew off its hinges. Wood splinters flew all over the place and filled the senses like a bad drug. Mimi screamed again, and I heard flesh hitting flesh. Rockets of pain, giving and receiving.

All went quiet.

I hopped off the bed and slipped into my boxers. Pants were usually required under these circumstances, but they would have put me at a competitive disadvantage. Agility was king when your life was on the line. Mimi might have dealt with a lot of bad dudes in her line of work, but I had dealt with worse.

These men were here for me.

I knelt behind the bed. Come a little closer, kitty kitty.

The footsteps went to the kitchen. Two sets of soles scuffing the hardwood. Two different dudes. I wasn't out of the woods yet. I knew that pride cometh before the fall, and I wasn't about to play hero. Scan your surroundings and make your move. Slow your breathing. Close your eyes. Then play the hand you've been dealt. Sal had taught me well. The average human clammed up under pressure. The nervous system triggered the adrenal glands which released ginormous doses of epinephrine.

Fight or flight.

And the average human always chose flight, like a wayward pigeon that never cared for the flock.

But I wasn't average.

I lowered myself onto my stomach and scooted under the bed. I knew that Mimi was down, but she wasn't out. I hadn't heard a gunshot, which meant she'd only taken a punch or kick or whatever the hell it was. When those hombres got to me, I'd greet them properly. And when I did, all bets were off. I could play the fight game, but I could play the street game too. Then I'd hightail it back to Vegas and make the suits happy.

The footsteps were joined by low, gravelly voices. Male. Assured. Dominant. A language I couldn't place. It sounded like they were swearing, but in the grand scheme of things who gives a shit.

Even bad dudes panic when they know what's coming around the corner.

The men flipped over couches and lamps and picture frames and paintings. They went into the guest bedroom and rinsed and repeated. My target theory was fading fast. Maybe Mimi had something top secret in the walls.

Twenty seconds later the men came into the master bedroom and knocked over Mimi's computer. I peeked out under the bed skirt and saw black Timberland boots with some blood on the wearer's right toe. I couldn't see the other pair. Normally I was respectful to guests, but today was a different story.

They'd hurt Mimi.

Enough of this shit.

I sprang out from under the bed—and was met by two guns pointed straight at my face.

So much for panic.

Both men wore black beanies and hoodies that ran down to their kneecaps. The whole ensembles were thrown off by green denim.

"Where're my toys?" I said.

"Get on the ground," Beanie 1 said. He spat on the carpet and flared his nostrils.

Beanie 2 had his gun trained on me, but he didn't say shit. Must have been Edgar's long-lost brother.

"This can go one of two ways," I said. "You get your asses kicked real fast. Or real slow." I stared them down.

Beanie 2 pistol-whipped me. My head throbbed and I felt blood trickling down my forehead.

Now we're talking.

I smiled.

"Where is it?" Beanie 1 said.

"I doth forget, madam."

I got pistol-whipped again.

"Wise guys get killed on these streets. Where the fuck is it?"

One of the benefits of having multiple guns pointed at your head is that things become crystal clear. No racking your brain for answers. No lollygagging. See it. Remember it. Spew it. Granted, I had no damned idea what the beanies were talking about, but I had an answer at the ready anyway. I was the Professor, and nobody was taking my crown.

"The prize you seek is in the nightstand," I said.

Beanie 2 furrowed his brow, and Beanie 1 did too. They stood there for a few seconds, lost in translation as if they were considering all the pros and cons of verifying my claim. I banked on the distraction. Distraction meant indecision, and indecision meant an opening.

My opening.

I bum-rushed Beanie 1 and tackled him into Mimi's desk. Beanie 2 fired a shot, but missed way right. I picked up Beanie 1 by the head, digging my fingers into his skull, and threw his ass right into Beanie 2. Newton's first law. An object in motion stays in motion unless acted upon by an unbalanced force. Beanie 1 and 2 fell like bowling pins.

And I went to work.

I stomped on their heads.

One.

Two.

One.

Two.

I kept a fluid rhythm as I took turns with the two of them. Tippity tap tap. I whistled while I worked. I couldn't quite get the tune right, but it's the effort that counts. Sal had given me all this for a rainy day. A fight outside the squared circle with its own fundamentals.

It's always raining around me.

The men writhed in pain, but I wasn't done. I picked up Beanie 1 and got him with two body shots to the kidneys. He was tougher than I gave him credit for, so I gave him another and he fell like a bag of sand.

"Where is it?" I said, mocking my quarry. I stuck my tongue out for good measure. I spit on them too. I wasn't a habitual spitter, but when the moment's right, the moment's right. It released all the tension and made things far more interesting.

Beanie 2 tried to play hero, but I connected with a left hook that sent him into next week.

Beanie 1 pushed himself back up. He was clearly the leader and the one with the most endurance.

"This can go a third way," he said. "We'll slit your fucking throat."

I found it amusing that he still had the ability to form coherent sentences, but that meant the job was far from over.

I grabbed his hair, pulling some out by the roots, yanked him straight up, and gave him a right uppercut. Then a left. I was ambidextrous. Right. Left. Right. Left. On the fourth combo, the man was counting sheep for a very long time.

Beanie 2 got up again, and I shook my head. *Stay down, hombre.*

He smiled. "Juko's gonna have a field day tonight."

I don't remember if it was the name that threw me, or the way he smiled with those yellow teeth, but all your opponent needs is half a second in the fight game. Waver and you'll be selling pancakes not consuming them.

Beanie 2 got me with a jab and a right hook to the body. He was a southpaw, so he threw with his right and got me off rhythm. I staggered back, woozy, but I shook the cobwebs off. When Beanie 2 charged, I blocked him, but then he got me with a knee to the stomach. There are no rules in the street fight game. Prepare for everything. *Expect* everything, dammit. Ain't no referees here.

Left hook.

Right hook.

Jab.

I threw all of it, and I hit air.

He kicked me to the ground and stood over me. "Boxers are the biggest pussies." He picked up his gun from where he'd dropped it and got ready to do the deed. A man can hope that he leaves this earth in a blaze of glory, Clint Eastwood-style. I was ready for my coronation.

But Mimi wasn't.

She clocked Beanie 2 with a perfect jab. Just the way I

taught her. Knuckle to flesh to skull. Beanie 2's eyes rolled into the back of his head and that's all she wrote.

Mimi took his gun and in one motion pointed in my direction and fired.

Beanie 1 had recovered, but some good that did. The bullet pierced his skull and his gun dropped to the floor. The asshole never got a chance to apologize.

I picked up his gun and realized that Henri and Bruce now both had killer parents. So much for peace and tranquility.

"Slow shot," I said.

"My ass," Mimi said.

We smiled.

Oxytocin is the best medicine sometimes.

But our moment was short-lived.

More footsteps entered the place, and then Finley appeared in the door.

"Drop your weapons," he said. "You're under arrest for murder."

30

Mimi got in the car first. Finley yelled some expletives and pushed her head into the back of his Ford Explorer. Then he came around the hood and squeezed my cuffs tighter.

"You're in for a real treat, champ."

"I hope it's a scrumptious one."

Finley punched me in the stomach and pushed me into the other side of the Explorer. The fix was in. I knew right then and there that Finley was the fink. It didn't take a rocket scientist to figure it out. How had he gotten to Mimi's place so quickly? The minute we dispatched the two bad hombres Finley showed like a damned ghost in heat. Unless he was camping with his radio under his arm, no way he could get there pronto.

But he was there.

Because he knew to be there.

Still, he wasn't calling all the shots. If he was, Mimi and I would be dead already. He would have left us on the bed, a tangled mess that screamed murder-suicide. He wouldn't play, and he'd make damned sure not a single print came back to him. He'd call in reinforcements to clean the place. Hell, he'd even replace the desk that one of the beanies broke. That was how it would have gone down.

No. Somebody else had told him to jump and Finley said how high. The powerbrokers had all the game while the minions pretended they did. They were lackeys, plain and simple. It didn't matter if one had a badge and was on the inside.

A fink was a traitor.

And the dictionary doesn't play favorites.

Finley was a traitor to his badge and his country and his community. And for what? Some cold hard cash. That was how it worked. A tale as old as time. Grease the po-po and they'll look the other way. Little by little, the cash becomes a hallucinogen. You need more to live more. You need more to keep the wife and kids happy. You need more to breathe more. I knew the score. Finley never called for backup, and as we were leaving the scene I didn't hear any sirens in the distance. No EMTs. No beat cops. No detectives. No cavalry.

Off the grid.

Just the way Finley wanted it.

Mimi had her head between her legs. I'd been in many cop cars, but this was Mimi's first time. If the cage separating officers from detainees didn't do it, then the smell sure as hell did. Vomit and piss and blood and a life unfulfilled. The mind is a fragile thing. Mimi sniffled and kept her head between her legs. She'd dealt with a lot of crazy hombres in front of the bench. Hell, she'd probably wanted to kill more than her fair share. But that was all talk. No action. It was an idiom. Kill them and be done with them. Figuratively speaking. But now that she'd actually gone through with the deed, Mimi was scarred for life. No other way around it. Maybe she had a superstar lawyer on speed dial since she ran in the same circles. I hoped for the best, but I expected the worst.

"You're not gonna make the fight," she said.

Damn.

I'd forgotten all about it amidst Finley's circus, but where there's a will there's a way.

"I'm not finished yet, princess."

Mimi lifted her head up and smiled at me.

I found love in the backseat of a cop car.

Finley picked up speed and had his oscillating lights on. I had no idea where the station was, but people like Finley didn't make it that easy. The station was out of the question. Finley would take us to a safe house and beat the shit out of us till his handler came. Movies were bullshit sometimes, but they were right on the money other times.

I looked out the window at the shrubbery that zipped past like an elongated version of Gumby. With each mile the green blended into the road, and at one point I thought Finley was gonna take us into the damned forest.

"You have no probable cause," Mimi said.

She knew there was a cage separating us from Finley, but she also knew that Finley heard right.

"Counselor, nobody gives a shit. What's a copper to do? Let two assholes get away with murder on his shift? And a celebrity on top of it. No sirree."

"The truth is a heavy burden that far few care to carry," I said.

"Ain't that right, champ? The truth is, you're not gonna make that fight tonight. And what a shame I had all that money riding on Juko. But ain't I the lucky one—when the commission recognizes your absence, you forfeit all your purse. And guess where it goes?" Finley paused for effect.

I didn't need the extra time.

"Juko gets all of it."

"Right on. You do have some brain cells left after all. Now let's really stump you. After Juko gets it, where does it go?"

I wanted to say *up your candy ass*, but that would have been too easy. It didn't go to me, that was for sure. Sims could fight that shit in the courts till he was in a rocking chair. Contracts are contracts.

"To charity," I said.

Finley made a buzzing sound with his lips. Or tried to. It sounded more like a hyena's swan song.

I said, "I got more lawyers than you have cojones."

Finley laughed. "Where you're going, ain't gonna be no lawyers."

Mimi's face went white. She started kicking the cage.

"Settle the fuck down," Finley said.

He blasted his radio and fiddled with the stations. He went from pop to country to news to pop and back to country. Then he abruptly went to a sports station. Some armchair wannabes were talking about the fight. We all listened for a few minutes. I was intrigued by their analysis, but ultimately unpersuaded. Juko had zero chance, and I'd show it soon.

I said nothing, but the Explorer did. The gears made some noises, but Finley ignored them. Which was too bad, because those problems would need to be addressed soon.

Finley said, "What kind of bologna they feed you all those years? Tyson or Trinity?" He grinned.

I studied the cage that kept me from knocking the shit out of him. Instead of an impenetrable polycarbonate, Finley's was black steel. Welded around the seating.

But not welded good enough.

Thousands of detainees had no doubt graced this backseat over the years, and some had naturally had issues with the cage. That made my job a hell of a lot easier.

My eyes flashed to Mimi's corner. The spot she'd kicked was dislodged just a little bit. Shitty governmental structures at their finest. I looked at Mimi, then at the cage, then at Mimi again. She got it right away. She was a counselor, after all.

Mimi kicked the cage again.

And I joined in.

Two lovers kicking a cage in the middle of some random highway in some random place in some random part of town.

Muy bueno.

Finley's traps rose all the way to his ears and he blasted the radio to the max. The pundits were giving their NFL picks for the upcoming season. Finley wanted to listen, but our kicks were pounding in his ears.

I wasn't exactly a physics major, but I knew that force times more force times more force times even more force eventually equals destruction. The cage would come down, come hell or high water.

And I was right.

Three minutes into our kicking fest, Mimi's side started to give. She let out a bloodcurdling scream and right when Finley looked back in her direction, I kicked the shit out of my side. The steel held its position for a second, then whipped straight into Finley's right ear.

Newton's law.

Finley screamed and lost control of the car. He veered to the right shoulder, grabbed the wheel, and flung it back in the direction of the road, but it was too late to right the ship. The Explorer had other plans. It flew off an embankment and crashed into a tree.

I saw stars.

Finley's airbag had deployed. He was fine.

But not for long.

I lunged through the open spot where the cage had been and I choked Finley with my cuffs.

31

Finley was game. He bit my right wrist and wouldn't let go. I choked him harder with the cuffs, and he chomped down deeper. A normal *Homo sapiens* would have broken the hold and caved to the external stimulus. Not me. Foul play is the fight game. You breathe it, smell it, taste it. Every round. If Finley was game, I was gamer.

But surprise is part of the fight game too. Finley pushed his feet up against the steering wheel and used every last bit of leverage to flip.

To the untrained eye, the flip wasn't the best choice given the circumstances. When the air is being forced out of you and you're seconds away from meeting your maker, gravity isn't on your side. Open the airway and live to fight another day.

But Finley must have been a gymnast in a prior life. I learned this the hard way. Right after he put his feet on the wheel and pushed off he contorted his body and caught my neck in a guillotine choke. Gravity plays no favorites, and something's gotta give. In that moment my forearms broke faster than the Bears' offensive line. Finley's legs were these big-ass tree trunks and he used them to his full advantage. He squeezed them together and laughed while smothering me.

"You little bitch," he said. "When you boxing pussies get in a real fight you know what's up."

I couldn't form full sentences. Lack of oxygen is no bueno. But actions speak louder than words.

I bit down on Finley's right thigh, and he broke the hold. As he grimaced and reached for his thigh, I hit him with the cuffs.

Like a battering ram.

One.

Two.

Finley blocked it on three, and we both tumbled out of the car.

Finley got up first, but I kicked his knee and he crumpled back down like a graham cracker.

Then he bounced back up.

We were three feet apart.

The copper and the captive.

Fair play.

Finley had balls after all.

This marked a first for me. I'd been in plenty of scrapes over the years. I relished kicking ass the way a suit relished collecting his fee. I'd fought with broken bones, bruised shins, dilapidated elbows, bulging discs, and a sleepy neck. I'd fought with one hand, and a bad one at that.

But I'd never fought with *no* hands.

Finley wanted to throw down, and I shared the sentiment.

I'd just have to do it with cuffs on.

"The ears are very sensitive organs," I said. "A cutman doesn't lie."

Finley sneered. "Appearances can be deceiving." He charged at me like a linebacker off the blocks. I sidestepped him and got him in the left ear with a sliver of my right cuff.

I could play defense with the damned things, but offense was a whole other matter.

I held up my cuffs. "Be a good lad and do away with these silly contraptions," I said. "My team won't forget it." I flashed my pearly whites, but Finley had been around plenty of cons over the years. His livelihood depended on bullshitting the bullshitters.

He smirked.

"Money's not all it's shaped up to be," Finley said. "You work your shift. Go home to the wife and kids. Dinner's on the table. Direct deposit every two weeks. Pension and deferred comp and health and vision. All the bells and whistles. But life's no cakewalk. The cars need fixing. The lawnmower needs a tune-up. The dog has a fistula."

I kicked Finley's right shin, but he blocked it like one of those Muay Thai dudes. Instead of countering, he danced back with his feet, mocking me.

"Shit happens," he said. "Comfort don't mean a damned thing anymore. Cancer is the dirtiest word in town."

"Preach," I said.

"My son, asshole. Hodgkins lymphoma. Doctors showed me charts and graphs and percentages. They talked cutting-edge treatments and therapies. The whole nine yards. You do what you gotta do for your kid. No questions asked. But when the wife gets laid off from the DMV and you've gotta pony up one hundred percent? Everything changes. You've gotta man up and save the day."

Finley spat at my feet.

"Nobody but ole Finley, you hear? My boy Edgar tried to help initially. Asked for an advance on his salary and got it. Edgar's got all the connects in all the right places. He gave and gave some more. But I have a conscience. I couldn't drain the rookie like that."

"He wears nicely pressed suits," I said.

Finley laughed and threw a punch.

I blocked it.

And we were back, three feet apart.

Shooting the shit.

"I see why you have such a following," Finley said.

"I'm a D-lister," I said.

"A what?"

I repeated myself, but this time Finley got me with a right hook straight to the left ear. I staggered back and heard seashells on the beach. Key West or some place. I shook the cobwebs off, but heard more seashells on more beaches.

Finley threw a jab, and I slipped it. He threw a right uppercut, and I bobbed and weaved out of harm's way. Defense was the best offense sometimes. As long as I kept my concentration, I could avoid bumps all day. Cuffs or no cuffs. Finley would hit air and I'd live to fight another day. But I knew that was futile. There comes a time in every fight, whether professional or amateur, when the stakes get raised. Some offhanded comment gets made. Some insult gets hurled. Some blasphemous image is put in somebody's mind that can't be taken back.

Then all bets are off.

And the big boys come out.

Coppers loved their metal power.

If Finley went for his gun, I was a goner.

So there was only one solution.

Keep exercising my maxilla.

What I do best.

I said, "'Tis a shame that the dinero didn't go your way. I take it you engaged in some form of police-sanctioned criminality to get all those Benjamins for treatment?"

Finley processed this for a second, then said, "Shut the fuck up, Gedrin. Juko was right. You don't know when to quit. And you failed the test earlier. After the challenger goes missing, forfeits his purse to the non-quitter, and the non-quitter gets the purse, where does it go then? It's a simple fucking question."

"Your boy's in for a long night after I'm done with him," I said.

Conventional wisdom said I had no chance of making the fight. Not in my condition. But wisdom and I had never made good bedfellows. I found a way. My way or the highway.

"I get it. You piece of shit. For all the work I did chaperoning a champ."

Finley pulled out his gun and fired. He missed a smidge left, the bullet ricocheting off the gravel. I wondered for a split second if it was a warning shot or if Finley was just a shitty shot, but I had more pressing matters. I tucked and rolled like a ninja, and Finley fired again and again, the bullets ripping dirt and missing their target. I got the hell out of Dodge. I heard Finley holster his gun and give chase. Branches broke with all his steps and all mine. He breathed like a wildebeest escaping a lion's jaws, and I breathed like a boss.

But I wasn't out of the woods yet.

I needed to adjust.

Now.

My eyes catalogued everything.

Left poplar.

Right azalea.

Center hydrangea.

Left hilly region.

Center ravine with water.

Bingo.

I ran toward the ravine and did a swan dive into it. It wasn't deep, so my knees bounced off the bottom right away.

But that gave me time.

Finley splashed in right after me.

"You couldn't just lay low. Sit it out. Have some fun. Fuck the lawyer and forget about the rest."

Finley threw a weak jab, and I slipped it and kicked him in the ribs. The wind was knocked out of his sails.

I said, "Four score and seven years ago, crooked cops ruled the roost." I kicked him again and again in the ribs, and he coughed up blood. Exploit your opponent's weakness till there's nothing left. "And no fucking way I'm eating bologna ever again, asshole."

I went for another kick, but Finley had my number.

He'd been playing me the whole time.

He caught my leg, twisted it, and pulled me under water. As he held my head down, bubbles broke to the surface faster than you can say hola. I couldn't hear what he was saying. I could see his bulky frame, but nothing more. And I discovered something. When you're about to drown, you think of pancakes and sex and that time you lost the spelling bee.

It all comes, fast and furious.

It takes the average human sixty seconds to drown. The brain gets deprived of oxygen and you go kaput. But that's without external forces. When you're being held underwater, the clock is cut in half. Twice. You're finished before you can describe your favorite pancake. My old cellie told me once. He'd been accused of such an act, beat the case, then managed to get picked up and hung out to dry on a different matter. Murder had all sorts of permutations.

I was seconds away.

My lungs felt like an ox's swing set.

Five.

Four.

Three.

Two.

Sorry, Sal.

One.

Finley's shape went away.

Zero.

My head was yanked out of the water. I grabbed at my throat, coughing out every last droplet of water. I saw double for a few seconds, then triple. Then everything went back to normal, and I saw Mimi. She had a gun in her hand, and no cuffs.

Finley's body floated in the water beside her.

"You're gonna miss your flight," she said.

32

Next thing I remember, I saw Nowa. I had no idea how he'd made it all the way to the Beaver State. He smiled and reached into the back of his boxy jeans. His hands moved in slow motion, like a freeze frame that was trying to figure itself out before being outed. I wish I could say that I clotheslined the hell out of him and made him bleed for all the shit that I'd been through the last forty-eight hours. He deserved it and then some. But no dice. The longer I stared at his pudgy hands, the more helpless I was. My mandible sat there like a bump on a log. My teeth felt like Elmer's glue and my feet had sand in them. I wasn't sinking, but I might as well have been. Stasis equals death.

Nowa had my number. He taunted me as his hand moved into his pocket. I couldn't see shit, and I'd had enough. I threw a jab and hit air. Then I threw a right hook and hit air again. Sometimes creativity is the best medicine. I lunged at Nowa like a jiujitsu hombre, and that's when it happened.

My body was frozen.

I sank into the ravine around me.

Nowa seized his moment and pulled out a Bowie knife. He licked the edges and sniffed the handle. He did this three times and muttered some Samoan words that I'd heard before but couldn't quite place now. Nowa was a linguist, and he would go toe to toe with Sal on many occasions. But even linguists meet their match.

I said, "Juko can't carry my jock."

Nowa smiled.

"Boy, there's no fight. There's never been a fight. The orderlies haven't told you? What happens in Vegas, stays in Vegas."

Before I could come up with a witty reply, Nowa threw the knife at me. It whistled past my right ear, taking off a bit of flesh. As I cupped my ear, Nowa threw another knife. Pockets were the best camouflage sometimes. The second knife took a bit off my left ear. I stood there, hands cupped, ears fucked, while the perp gloated.

Then I heard boots splashing the water behind me. Slowly. Slowly. Slowly. The hubbub of pre-conflict. If this were a spaghetti western, I'd describe it as the moment when the hay rolls through the town and the occupants run indoors and take up seats in the gallery.

To watch the shit show.

One.

Two.

Three.

Step.

Step.

Step.

On four, the cowboy showed himself.

"The lawman never dies," Finley said. He sneered and flashed his teeth. They were gangrene now and his gums were the only thing left on the menu.

"Fuck you," I said.

I uncupped my hands from my ears. Blood poured out like a fountain. But I didn't care. I threw rights and lefts and lefts and rights.

Nada.

My feet were slipping.

I needed out fast.

But it was too late.

Finley walked over to me and ran his gun along my thigh, teasing me like Magrece at Toots. He made his way up my chest to my jaw, hovered the gun under my chin for a bit, then scraped my nose. He ran his finger over the trigger, then pulled back.

"A con doesn't belong out on these streets," he said. "You spend your whole life protecting and serving and they wanna rise up and make a name for themselves. Shame."

In that moment he was the biggest heel I'd ever seen.

"Any last words, sonny?"

There comes a time in every man's life when he ponders his own mortality. Not the fact of mortality. That's a given. But the actual nitty-gritty details. The how and the when and the where. I'd pictured it earlier and now I pictured it again. A grand tour de force. I'd go out guns blazing. That's the way I wanted it. If you could script your own mortality.

But life throws curveballs better than the Rocket.

"Pancakes," I said.

Finley fired the gun right into my chest.

And everything went black.

"Easy there," Sims said.

My eyes flew open.

I was on a long leather couch, looking at my toes. I wasn't wearing socks. And when I looked up, I saw Sims's mean mug.

"You've been knocked out for the last hour," he said.

"That's what you get when you're chasing pussy instead of titles."

I shook off the cobwebs and realized I was back on the PJ.

"Pleasure comes in many forms," I said.

"And not one word about that cop. He was so crooked his own partner ratted him out to the feds. Been building an investigation for months. Edgar cleared all this shit up and they're looking at it as a suicide instead of a multiple-defendant party."

"You lawyers always have the right words."

"When I said you weren't going back in, I meant it. You have unfinished business."

"With my bed. Don't wake me. Even if my sleepwalking game is on point. Kick my ass back to sleep."

Sims rolled his eyes, but that meant all was well again. We were constantly on the outs and the ins and the outs and the ins, but it was all in good fun. When push came to shove, we found the ins like all brothers do. He'd changed my life back before my fall from grace, and he'd fixed it afterward. I couldn't hate the man no matter how much I tried sometimes. My happiness always involved a dose of Sims. Add a dose to the beaker and rinse and repeat.

"Where's Sal?" I didn't want any more theatrics.

Sims shook his head. "He's at the arena. A parking attendant gave him shit about not having credentials, but he challenged the guy to a pushup contest and got in eventually."

"What was the score?"

"Forty to thirty-three."

"Sal's a monster."

"The fucking guy is one stubborn mule." Sims laughed.

"Security?" I asked.

"Extra tight. Nobody in or out of the bubble of the locker room. Not taking any chances this time."

"I feel like shit."

"Kick Juko's ass and you can take some time off. You up for it?"

It was the first time he'd ever asked me how I was feeling. Not the business shit like how do you feel about this cereal box or these boxers or this razor. The basic, human shit. The platitudes and marching orders came with the territory on fight weekend, but the basic human shit meant Sims had a soul after all. I thought he was an alien, but even aliens are full of surprises.

I closed my eyes to get some sleep, but it was short-lived.

"Hell yeah he's up for it. He's one tough cookie," Mimi said.

A leather recliner swiveled around to reveal her sitting there, and she raised her hands as if to say "ta-da." I wanted to critique her form, but I bit my tongue. A man never criticizes a woman's twirl when the equipment on board isn't up to snuff. The recliner wasn't as comfy as the couch.

"He's gotta go twelve rounds," Sims said.

"Not a chance in hell," I said. "One's the magic number."

Sims waved me off and went to the back of the jet to play agent some more.

Mimi got up and sat next to me on the couch. "Green tea? It's filled with antioxidants," she said.

"I'm good."

She rubbed my shoulders, in a tender way.

"What's the game plan?"

"How are you?" I asked.

Mimi stopped. "I was worried back there, but you pulled through."

"I mean the men. Two lives is two lives."

Mimi sat in silence for several seconds. I knew she was thinking of the lives she'd taken. It wasn't her fault, but the normal mind goes on an emotional rollercoaster and doesn't let up. Taking a life was no bueno. Still, at the end of the day in a dog-eat-dog world, if you're not on top you're in the dirt.

Mimi buried her shoulder into my chest and cried. "My hands are stained with their blood forever."

I put a hand on her back. "You rid the world of two smelly assholes."

She sniffled and then laughed, and eventually wiped her tears. "All right, mister, get focused."

"Yes, ma'am. See target. Beat the shit out of target. Muy simple."

Mimi kissed me, and I kissed back. It went like that for several seconds till she broke first.

She pulled back. "And when you win, I might just give you a present."

"Put a bow on it, missy, and I'm game."

Mimi shook her head.

Truth be told, having a female companion on the same wavelength as you is one of the finer things in life. It doesn't happen all that often, so when it does you have to cherish it and live every second in the moment.

I stared at Mimi for a few seconds, saying nothing at all. Then I moved my mandible.

"It means a lot that you're here," I said.

"I know." She took my hand and massaged small circles around my knuckles. "I like you a lot."

"Same."

But there was more.

Mimi said, "To be honest, there's a lot I *don't* like though. Sometimes I feel overwhelmed and need a breather around this adventure ride."

She took her hand away and went back to the swivel chair.

33

J uko grinned like a Cheshire cat backstage. He wore blue trunks and a yellow t-shirt with a lizard on it from some cola company. He had blue wraps on, but not his gloves. He had no idea that I was in the building.

He'd banked on Finley and Nowa and that Toots cowboy man to take me down.

Yeah, right.

One of the sharks said, "Talk about your journey to this fight."

Juko had been ready for this moment his whole life. "I've been in the ring since I was ten years old. Bobbing, weaving, slipping. You name it, I've done it from the jump. While all the other kids were fooling around and playing video games, I was working to chase my dream. Heavyweight champion of the world."

The shark feigned that he actually cared. "You must be disappointed that this big fight for the number one contendership is on the verge of going up in flames. My sources tell me Gedrin's not in the building yet and it's been reported that with his Portland legal troubles he may not make it. His purse is in jeopardy too."

Juko knew all this already, but he played it cool. "Gedrin's troubles are his own making. I'm here prepping to go to war and he's out there talking to judges and attorneys over stupid shit that's he done in his life. This is a pure sport. This is a respect game. You either have it or you don't. So many greats have come before us and when somebody like Gedrin pulls shit like that, he spits on their graves. Stop the theatrics. Let's fight. And that purse? I hear I get it if he pussies out and doesn't show. I'll take a little extra cash and then go win my title."

You ain't getting shit, junior.

Juko was right about one thing though. Theatrics did tend to sidetrack things. But they also made the game and built the name of all those legends he talked about. The fans lived for the shit show. Hence the press conference that did crazy ratings, thanks to *moi*.

Juko jumped rope.

The shark reporter smiled. "I'm told that if Gedrin's not in the building for glove check in the next ten minutes, the fight is officially off."

Juko shed crocodile tears. "You work so hard in life, and to have it all taken away because of some dumbass is really sad. I hope the promoters never give that quitter a title shot. Gedrin the prideful bitch."

He went back to his jump rope and the reporter took several steps back. The camera zoomed in on Juko's abs as he counted his reps. Off camera I could hear Nowa yelling.

But enough was enough.

Time for more theatrics, hombre.

I looked at Sims, and he looked at Sal. Sal walked out of the locker room and shouted something down the hall. Then he turned back, banged on the door like it was an ashiko, and smiled. I don't remember his exact words, or if they were even in English, but he got the job done. Where there's a shark, there's always a frenzy.

A drove of reporters pushed into the locker room with their camera teams. They flipped their lights on, but I was still glued to the big screen.

Juko's interview.

Juko said, "Game over. Who's the bitch now?"

Then the reporter beside him tapped his ear a couple times, and smiled. He'd gotten the news and was relishing the moment he got to reveal it.

"I'm getting word that Gedrin is in the building. He's standing by in the locker room."

The reporter wanted another comment, but he didn't need one. A picture is worth a thousand words. Juko's face was alabaster white.

Look who's back, asshole.

The sharks in front of me went live and hurled a bunch of questions. They asked about my case, my face, my stamina, and more. I wasn't in the mood for giving many answers, so I struck a happy medium. I answered three questions, and I answered the rest of the questions with questions of my own. Rhetorical questions were the best game in town. I did that for six minutes straight. At one point Sal groaned and I knew that was my cue to hang it up.

I had a fight to win, after all.

But I knew the score better than the sharks knew their cages.

A soundbite.

Always end with a soundbite.

I looked smack dab in the camera and said, "To all the haters out there, enjoy tonight, because it's the last time you'll ever see Juko alive."

The sharks ate it up.

Then Sal shouted at them and they shut their cameras off and left the locker room. When they were gone, Sal picked up the wraps.

"We're gonna kill him now?"

"Always give the fans what they want," I said. "They paid for your son's school."

Sal shook his head. "That he quit after one semester to work at the gym. The *stupido*. Boyo, this one is gonna come down to the cards. You hear?"

I nodded, but I knew and Sal knew that I was a runaway train when I got in the ring. Everything Sal said went in one ear and out the other as I walked my opponent down. I wasn't going for a decision. The judges' scorecards were the dirtiest in town. They were worse than stale mayo on stale bread on stale meleagris. If I wanted my title shot, I'd have to put that punk ass down for good.

Sims called in the checker, and he looked on as Sal did my wraps. There were all sorts of rules and all sorts of anxieties in the fight game. Back in the day fighters used to slip knives and other contraptions in the wraps, and it turned out horribly. So the invasion of privacy before the fight was out of my control. Show those hands.

After the wraps, Sal put on the gloves. The checker kept watching, but there was nothing to see. I usually went with light green or light blue. But since this was the first time in a while, I went with a special edition that looked a little like the madam's hair at Toots. The checker signed off on the whole ensemble and left the locker room.

That left me, Sal, Sims, and Mimi.

She was in the corner on her phone, taking selfies and uploading them to some clouds. I'd heard her saying the term many times over the last hour and had no clue what the hell she was talking about. I was tempted to ask her for all the nitty-gritty details, but some things were best left unsaid. I hadn't brought up the talk from the PJ, but for now that was on the back burner. I had a job to do, and dammit, I wasn't going to let Henri down. He expected to live in doggy excess.

I jogged in place and Sal shouted a bunch of instructions. Sims talked to some more suits, then left the locker room.

"Boyo," Sal said, "I'm proud of you."

"Hold your tongue, viejo. I might go down with the ship. I'm over the hill. My bones ain't what they used to."

"Cut that shit. You've been ready for this fight since the minute you went in."

I nodded. "It'll be hell to pay."

Mimi looked up from her phone. "You better listen to him, Lance. You have trouble doing that."

Sal shook his head at her. "You're too smart for this *idiota*. Trade up, my dear, and quickly."

Mimi smiled and went back to the clouds.

Sal put on the mitts, and we went to work for a few minutes. We usually did ten minutes of mitts before we got into position for our entrance. A great entrance made the main event sometimes. More theatrics. It's a science, dude.

But we never made it.

Mimi screamed.

And Bentini said, "One more step, and I slit her fucking throat."

34

If I had a dollar for every time my significant other was put in harm's way because of my significant stupidity, I'd be a millionaire ten times over. No broken knuckles or noses or shins needed. No CTE either. I could kiss the fight game goodbye and Sims could move on to rep prim and proper tennis players.

But pipe dreams were pipe dreams for a reason.

Bentini wasn't playing games. He socked Mimi right on the forehead and held the knife square against her throat. He kicked the back of her knees for show, and when she buckled to gravity, he propped her back up and grinned like the Joker.

"All my life, I've been waiting for the day when I could defeat the impenetrable Lance Gedrin." His eyes grew wide and his jaw clenched. "Always calling the shots. The man of the hour. A million guys on his payroll. The saint. The charity man."

Mimi had a blank expression on her face. Maybe she'd faced down thuggish clients before, or maybe after the Finley fiasco she'd come to terms with her mortality. I wanted to reassure her, but I needed an opening.

I stared Bentini down, biding my time. I knew that he wouldn't kill his quarry with this many witnesses. He wasn't stupid enough to do that. He'd taunt and cajole and ridicule and proselytize till he got his wish. Even the dumbest kid in the back of the class could figure it out now. Bentini wanted me to quit. He wanted me out of the fight. He wanted me to lie down.

Bentini was in on the grab, plain and simple. Him. Finley. Nowa. The three musketeer wannabes conspired to take me down with a panoply of obstacles that would make the Monopoly man jealous. Bullshit followed by bullshit followed by even more bullshit. A maze of epic proportions.

For money is the root of all evil.

But what Bentini didn't realize was that I had nothing to lose. Mimi and I were great, but when you're put through the wringer and come within seconds of death courtesy of the government and non-government, life takes on a whole new meaning. You make a bucket list and smile more and breathe more and respect all the fine moments in life you otherwise would have made short shrift of. And in those moments, in the silence, you don't lose focus. You're at your peak state. Some call it flow. Others call it being high on adrenaline.

I called it fucking awesome.

So while Bentini had been planning his ambush for quite some time, focus meant spontaneity. And spontaneity meant something even greater.

Uncertainty.

Boy, how I loved uncertainty.

I always came through in the clutch.

Opening, opening, on the wall, when is the best moment of them all?

Every plan called for that one turn-of-the-tide moment.

The hero is down on the mat, blood pouring down his forehead like Niagara Falls. All is lost. Doubt creeps in. Tears form for a second, then stop. Memories flood the cerebellum. The eyes become cloudy. But the opening can be as simple as a smile or a snicker or a pupil losing focus for half a second. The turn of the tide wasn't uniform, and it couldn't be precisely measured.

But I knew it when I saw it.

Counselors don't back down.

Mimi kicked Bentini in the balls, and I charged him. Bentini was ready with the knife, and he got me with three circular cuts on my right shoulder. They were grazing cuts, but blood is blood.

I threw a hard right, and my glove hit air.

I went for a left uppercut and my glove bounced off the knife like a trampoline. I was lucky as hell that my glove provided me all that cushion for this crazy-ass hombre.

"I should have fed you to the monkeys," Bentini said. "But that would have been too nice."

"I'm friends with the monkeys. Henri, too."

Bentini threw a left uppercut that got my left shoulder. I shouldn't have felt it, but in the fight game it's the cumulative damage that does you in. From cowboy man to Finley to fucking Bentini, keep taking shots and adios amigo. Bentini knew this. He'd been in my corner for years. He'd catalogued all the mind games and all the cheap shots and all the chicanery. And to think he was once a pizza delivery boy.

I got him with a right hook, but Bentini got me with a right body shot. My abs felt like slabs of icicles ready to meet the sun. I didn't realize then that Bentini was still blocking shots with the knife. He parried and parried and came back stronger. He was a machine, and no doubt he'd been practicing while I was at Pontiac making friends.

Sal shouted in the background, and as always when the fight was on, so was my tunnel vision.

Just me and Bentini.

One on one.

Mano a mano.

Just bring it.

"Finish up kiddo, so I can waste your boy." I spit at Bentini's feet and he came back with the knife, but hit air. My defense was on point.

"Leave a note and let the fish come to pasture," he said. "I knew your stupid ass would follow the trail all the way through. Follow the crumbs. Follow the cheese. A rat doesn't know what's good for it till it gets that shock therapy. The sea parted, and here comes Investigator Gedrin. Too bad you didn't bring that badge from that piece-of-shit show of yours. Souvenirs really improve the vibe."

"Come closer and I'll shove the badge up your ass. Let's be clear. For the vibe."

Bentini swung again with the knife, hitting air. I danced a little and did some head bobs. Sal shouted something again, but I couldn't hear him.

"One minute you're on top of the world, stopping bleeds for the champ. Next, you're selling SIM cards and pizza for the morbidly obese. And did I ever get a thank-you for my services? Did I ever get a thank-you for stopping the blood so that you could win? Remember Goluka? Asshole, I'm not talking about the belt. He tagged you with seven seconds left in the first. That shit was pooling like the Pacific. Sal bought a few extra seconds with the ref, I worked my magic, and voila—you keep going. That cut never opened again and you won the title."

"Cuts are your cup of tea," I said.

"That's your fucking problem," Bentini snapped. "It's all a big joke to you. It's not easy putting the damned kids through college. One day you have insane dough, the next no dough. Wifey wanted to murder me."

"Nowa would have brought you on in a heartbeat."

"Nowa's balls are even smaller than yours, and he's a frugal bitch."

I firmly disagreed on the whole concept, but I found our little chat highly entertaining. Plus, the more he chatted the less focused he was on plunging a knife into me.

"Yet he joined your pity parade and was no longer Team Gedrin," I said.

Bentini scowled. "The minute you got out, we knew your greed would take over. You wanted that green and were gonna do anything to get it. We laid low while you fucked things up in Chicago, then when Sims got the fight through, we had our opening. For life. But none of it would be possible without somebody on the inside. With a real badge and real power."

"Finley."

"Yes. You are learning. He wanted to help his kid and owed Nowa after he tipped him off to a huge drug ring at the gym last year. But a promotion is never enough for a crooked cop."

"I share your sentiment, hombre." I threw a right hook, but Bentini blocked it with the knife and we were back to square one. Dancing and talking just like old times. Only Bentini was tougher than the last time we'd sparred.

"All you had to do was stay in Portland. Keep your head down. Fully rest up. Live to fight another day. Work on yourself. All that self-empowerment shit. Instead, things had to get a tad bit physical."

"I thoroughly appreciate it," I said.

"Fuck you," Bentini said.

"Your penmanship is putrid."

"Ah, the cog in the wheel. Parson. You're not as smart as I thought, Gedrin. Everybody has a number."

"Fink," I said.

"Absolutely. Sing it to me, boy. You had all the time in the world to make amends and now you're crying wolf. There's only one traitor. *You're* the fink, asshole."

Bentini charged at me. And this time I'd had enough playing by Nevada's rules.

I sidestepped him and kicked him right in the face.

Bentini went down like a sack of potatoes. But the hombre was made of steel. He hopped back up and threw ridiculous combos, channeling his dad.

Hook.

Body shot.

Jab.

Uppercut.

Hard right.

I blocked a few and I ate a few. I staggered back and then went right for his weakest link.

The ribs.

He dropped the knife and went down again.

He tried to hop back up, but I pinned his shoulders with my boots.

"Finks aren't family," I said. I pounded Bentini's face till it resembled a mashup of the Smashing Pumpkins and the Beatles. He screamed in a bunch of languages I didn't understand and he prayed in a bunch of others.

But I wasn't done.

I grabbed the knife and was ready to finish the job, but Mimi stopped me.

"Enough! Please."

I dropped the knife and saw her for the first time. I really *saw* her.

She had her hands over her mouth and tears streamed down her cheeks, smearing her makeup.

This wasn't her life.

This was mine.

And it was here to stay. Violence and blood and power and thirst.

The road less traveled.

I couldn't blame her.

Then Sal slapped me in the head. "You should have finished that punk earlier. Soft like his daddy. When you see the knife, you don't see the knife. Got it, boyo?"

I didn't. Sal treated my wounds, and then Sims ran in with a bunch of security guards.

I pointed to Bentini, and Sims pointed to Sal. Instead of pointing at Mimi, Sal lifted the collar of his shirt up and pulled out a little recording device. The old man had gotten it all on tape. He tossed it to Sims.

Muy bueno.

Then Sal got down to business.

"Showtime," he said.

I smiled. "One fink left."

35

I felt eighty percent on my game. With all the hoopla over the last couple days I'd be lying if I said I was completely in the zone. But the beauty of talent is that you can get away with things that the non-talented can't. Juko was well-rested and well-prepared. He didn't have a scratch on him. Physically or emotionally.

But he wasn't the champ.

I was.

I never lost my belt.

Sal tapped my shoulders like a drum behind the curtain and gave me a pep talk. I smiled and nodded at all the right times. I couldn't recite Sal's speech from memory, but it was good enough that it focused me in on the task at hand. No frills and simple in scope. Kick Juko's candy ass. I was the best and I knew it. Hell, everybody in the world knew it. I visualized my target and smiled.

Juko's music hit, and the crowd cheered. Vegas always had a bipartisan crowd, but appearances were deceiving sometimes.

I jogged in place and stretched my neck. I threw some jabs and slipped imaginary fists.

Then *my* music hit, and the crowd went wild. Fuck Juko and his crowd. A fighter's music is part performance and part beautiful musicality. Tyson came to the ring with one eerie drop tone that elevated heart rates and pulses with the best of them. When he faced off, the fight was already over.

I was a firm believer in multiple tones.

Two, to be exact.

An Irish rhythm and a fiddler's fancy.

I came out of the curtain with Sal on my left and Sims on my right. The lights were flashing, and the HBO camera crew was tracking my movement, taking care not to slip and fall on live television. Behind me, a bunch of security honchos in red escorted me to the ring. If all hell broke loose, they were my protectors. Which was hilarious in every sense of the word. I didn't need a protector back in the locker room, and I sure as hell didn't need a protector out here. If things got messy I'd be the first one in on the action, and I'd use my pythons till the cows came home.

I got to the ring and Juko stared me down, pacing side to side.

Bring it on, hombre.

He was scared shitless in back, but now he was putting on the show for the cameras. Pride cometh before the fall. Nowa rubbed his boy's shoulders and slapped him on the chest to get him in the game.

I got through the ropes, and I was home.

I pumped my fist for the crowd.

I rubbed my boots against the canvas.

I stood on the turnbuckle, kissed my gloves, and held my hands out like I'd just won all the heavyweight belts in the game.

Sal hated this pre-fight shit, but this shit sold the fight and made me a household name all those years ago. I wasn't stopping now.

We were seconds away.

Sims said something annoying to me, then Sal gave me another pep talk, then Michael Buffer announced us all to the world.

And then the first round started.

We felt each other out, throwing jabs that never landed. I threw five jabs and Juko threw six. Sal wanted me to throw one jab and feel Juko out for the rest of the round, but in my eyes five jabs wasn't nearly enough. I threw three more and hit air.

Then the bell sounded.

End of Round 1.

Juko shook his head and pounded his chest as he went back to his corner.

Sal slapped my ear when I got back to mine.

"Test his jab out. Get him off balance, boyo. You don't need to play hero."

My new cutman took my mouthguard out and I spit into a bucket that might have been in vogue during the Jurassic Park days. The cutman worked his magic, even though there wasn't anything to work. I was fresh. I made a note to keep him on if he wasn't a stabber.

And then we got going again.

Round 2.

Juko came out hard. He got me with a left jab, then a small right body shot. A minority of the crowd cheered, while the rest of the crowd stayed silent. They knew the score. Once I got going, adios amigo.

It's hard to say when I decided to turn it on. I wish I could say that I pre-planned it—that I listened to my trainer.

Hell no.

Something itched in my decrepit brain cells and that gave me all the jolt I needed. Sometimes the itch came slowly, other times it came like a lion's roar. And that's all she wrote.

This time it came like a lion's roar.

I got Juko with a body shot to the left rib cage, but he countered with a body shot of his own.

He walked me into a corner and got me with two clean jabs, and Sal was screaming so hard from the corner I thought he was gonna pop a lung out.

Then it happened.

I saw it.

Not Sal.

Not Sims.

Not Mimi.

But Leroy.

I saw his chiseled face and his crooked smile and his wife and his kids and his legacy.

And Leroy's words reverberated through me like the percussion of a massage gun.

Throw that body shot twice.

He's too full of shit to play defense.

Get that motherfucker.

For me.

I smiled, and Juko raised his brows.

I threw a hard body shot to his right kidney.

Bam.

It rocked him.

I threw it again.

BAM.

Juko staggered back, and all of Nowa's fancy training and crooked connections couldn't save his boy. Juko threw a hard right. I slipped it and hit him so good with a right hook that he was re-learning the alphabet.

Left uppercut.

Jab.

Right kidney.

Left kidney.

Juko fell back into the corner and I walked him down.

Home is home.

The crowd roared, and with each roar, I did too.

Right, left, right, left, right, left.

Juko's face would make for a great Picasso on the wall.

And then it happened.

Juko's eyes rolled into the back of his head. He was punch-drunk, and when somebody is punch-drunk they make their final play.

But their legs are like Jell-O and that play, while brazen, is both pathetic and futile.

Juko tried to clinch me.

I threw him off and got him with one of the best uppercuts I'd ever thrown in Sin City.

Juko went down like a lead balloon.

KO.

Round 2.

One minute in.

Sal stormed the ring and kissed the top of my head. He flicked off Nowa, who was sulking in his corner. Medics tended to Juko while a mob of security and cameras invaded the ring.

Michael Buffer announced my name again as the winner.

Then I did media.

My statement was crystal clear. I'd been preparing it for quite some time. But there's always room for more.

Sims forgot my guitar, so I took one of the shark's mics and belted out "YMCA" with all the hand gestures. Sal didn't expect my song choice, and that's what made him join the party. He mixed up a couple of the letters, but it was one hell of a moment.

Then I walked to the center of the ring and said, "I lost over twelve years of my life for something I didn't do. But I never lost hope. Every day I trained and dreamed of this. Standing before all of you, kicking ass. This is my ring. I'm the champ, champ. I'm ruthless, I'm unstoppable. Then, now, forever. Juko gave it everything he had, but you gotta bring more to the game when you're boxing with God. And that poser with my belt better count the days. 'Cause he gone. Where he at?" I looked around the ring for the supposed champ. He'd already left. He and his team didn't want any of this. "I'd like to dedicate this win to Leroy, my cornerman who couldn't make it out. I'm with you, brotha."

I blew kisses to the crowd, and they erupted.

I was asked questions about my next fight and my next trip and all sorts of other miscellaneous oddities, but I simply gave the mic to Sims so he could earn his pay.

When I turned, Mimi was in the ring.

"I see why you love this shit," she said. "It's addicting."

She kissed me.

36

Fifteen hours later I was at Horseshoe Bend. The world
has many majestic views, and the wizened traveler
makes a point to experience every last one of them.
Time moves on, but memories last forever. The Bend had been
on my bucket list from the minute I went inside. It damned
near stood at the top of the list, but potatoes got in the way.
Situated in Page, Arizona, with views of the Colorado River
that would make a king jealous, the Bend is quite simply a
geological masterpiece. The word is that eons ago the rivers
flowed and got trapped in their beds. When the waters met a
sandstone escarpment, the result was a two-hundred-seventy-
degree bend in the river. The Jitterbug couldn't do the place
true justice. Luckily Mimi had a fruit phone with multiple
cameras on it.

I took in the gorge while Henri and Bruce played tug of war
with an orange rope. Henri had come a long way in the last
couple months, and I was a proud fur padre. He played with
care, comfort, and control. At times he ceded the rope to his
playing companion and at others he ran away with it. But he

always brought it back. It was a beautiful sight to behold. Canine bliss without a care in the world. Henri was a good citizen after all.

Mimi took some pics of the Bend. "I'll send these to you. What's your email?"

"Maple syrup at gmail dot com," I said. "Or you could just send them to my phone."

Mimi laughed.

"Your phone is on its last legs."

"Not in a million years." The Jitterbug didn't jibe with modern artistry and decor, but it could still go, go, go. What was wrong with it? Absolutely nada. "I'll text you Sims's number."

"Sims do your laundry too?"

"No way. I have sensitive skin so no fancy softeners for me, missy. I rebel when the time and place is right."

Mimi smiled.

It'd been one hell of a ride the last couple days, but all rides reach their destination eventually. The question becomes whether it be mutual or acrimonious. Mimi and I had made our decision in bed after the fight. We stayed up all night and dissected it from every angle. Mimi went first and I went last. Then we talked about it some more on the ride over to the Bend. We had a connection, but sometimes timing is everything.

She was in a Portland high-rise. I was usually in a new motel in a new state in the Union. She was a counselor. I was a brain surgeon. Maybe one day the stars would align and we'd go on more adventures together, but for now it was adios, amigo.

We decided to mutually part ways.

"Back to the criminals tomorrow?" I said.

"Bench trial at ten. Motion at eleven. Bond hearing at noon. Lighter than usual." She shook her head.

"Keep working on that jab. You've got potential."

"Thanks." She pulled me close and gave me a long kiss. I should have timed it because by the end my mouth was numb from all the fun.

Then Henri barked and Bruce joined in.

We broke.

"You're really something, Gedrin," Mimi said.

"Gracias."

"I've had more excitement this weekend than I've had my whole life."

"Curiosity killed the cat."

"Shut up."

"Come here."

I pulled her in and held her even longer than our kiss.

Then we broke again and Mimi took more shots of the gorge. The sun shone brighter and glistened off the sedimentary rock. Some called it natural beauty and others called it man-made excess and greed. I was cool either way. Life's a riot, no matter how you slice it.

Officially, I was the number one contender in the world. Sal's cachet was better than ever. Nowa's gym would close down soon. And Leroy was not only back and feeling good, he was demanding to be in my corner for the title fight. I wasn't quite at the top of the mountain, but I was damned close.

I didn't know when I'd get it all back, but in that moment it was honestly the last thing on my mind.

"Are you hungry?" I said.

Mimi raised an eyebrow. "Are you treating me to a farewell brunch, champ?"

"Hell yeah."

Mimi smiled.

And we got pancakes.

AUTHOR'S NOTE

Thanks for reading! I hope you enjoyed the Gedrin universe just as much as I enjoyed writing it. I would greatly appreciate it if you would leave a review on Amazon. Reviews allow more readers to find Gedrin, and this ultimately allows me to keep writing stories that I hope will leave an indelible footprint in our literary world.

—Greg

ACKNOWLEDGMENTS

Thank you to my team. Writing may be a solitary endeavor, but publishing is certainly a collective one. Thank you to my beta readers Bailee Myers and Miranda Niles. Your early insights really helped whip Gedrin into shape.

Thank you to my editor David Gatewood for making my prose shine. Thank you to my proofreader Donna Rich for snagging those pesky typos. Thank you to my cover designers at Deranged Doctor Design. I'm blown away by all the Gedrin covers and this one is no different.

And of course thank you to all those who have shaped my writing indirectly in some way. It's impossible to mention everybody here, but y'all know who you are.

ALSO BY GREG GOUNTANIS

THE LANCE GEDRIN SERIES

The Night Contract (Lance Gedrin #1)

The Fink (Lance Gedrin #2)

The Loran (Lance Gedrin #3)

The Jobber (Lance Gedrin #4)

The Lance Gedrin Box Set (Books 1-4)

SNEAK PEEK THE LORAN (GEDRIN #3)

I'm a hooker. When carbon steel collides with the urethane sphere in front of my feet, sidespin rules the roost. Thousands of RPMs taunt me as the white dimples take off opposite their intended line. A hooker can make a variety of changes: grip, ball position, stance, weight at address. But at the end of the day, it all means shit.

Golf is a Jekyll and Hyde game.

One minute you're king, and the next you're that kid who fucks up the word "received" at the spelling bee. Mechanics are the real deal, and the fine details make or break the game. One degree variance in club face position at impact meant your shot would fly two yards off line.

The average amateur is off several degrees.

I learned all this as a sophomore in high school, carrying a bag of wooden brassies around the links. I'd take in the luscious greens, the slanting tee boxes, the slippery bunkers, and I'd hack my ball around the slopes. I'd keep score in my head, and I quickly learned that a professor was required to play the game at a high level. Study the angles and the centrifugal forces and there was a sliver of hope you'd make a name for yourself.

So while the other kiddos would boast about getting laid and swiping whiskey from their parents' lake house, I'd boast about nailing slick six-footers downhill with a left-to-right break. I'd rave about the nuances of bent grass greens and blue-grass and Poa annua. Stimpmeter was my middle name, and five-hour rounds were bliss.

But all good things come to their natural end.

In my case, I realized that my true talents lay elsewhere. I couldn't eagle a damned hole, but the moment I stepped foot in Sal's boxing gym I was walking on air. Fully approved warfare. Blood, sweat, and tears. Pure, unabashed chaos. I donned the gloves, and the first time I sparred I bashed somebody's brains in. Nobody could touch me.

So I traded in my clubs and I never looked back. I rose up the ranks faster than you could say *hola*. Every promoter wanted me on their card, and it wasn't long before I became the undisputed heavyweight champ. I would have kept my title, too, if it wasn't for the fact that I was wrongfully convicted of murder. Twelve years in the slammer before I was sprung by my lawyer, who was moonlighting as a serial killer—literally.

Such is life.

Now, I don't bring all this up for pity points. I call balls and strikes better than anybody. I bring all this up because it's fucking obvious that you can't improve your swing in a seven-by-eleven cell with zero equipment and a bunch of hombres trying to shank you after hours. Which explains why my first round of golf in roughly two decades was no bueno.

I stood now on the eighteenth tee at Rainmaker Golf Club in Alto, New Mexico. Freedom is a beautiful thing. I'd wanted to get back out there and see if muscle memory was real. The sun peeked out over the canyons, and when the clouds parted, the ambience was something straight out of a magazine. My agent, Mark Sims, had pulled some strings and gotten me a tee time right at civil twilight. I'd started the round with a glow-in-the-dark golf ball and plenty of shitty swings, but my game steadily improved on the front nine, and I was on pace now to shoot even par on the back.

If I parred eighteen.

I analyzed the hole and knew that it called for a cut. It was a dogleg right par five. I was playing from the middle tees, and there was no chance in hell I'd be able to reach in two shots. Hell, I'd reached a par five in two just once in my golfing life, and that was because a seagull played favorites one time, picked up my ball, and dropped it on the green. I'd proceeded to four-putt that hole. The course giveth and the course taketh away.

There were no seagulls in sight today. This hole would need three good swings to get on the green. The problem with being a hooker was that while the ball did end up getting more carry than it would with a fade, the ball also had much more sidespin, and sailed out of bounds quite frequently. So I pictured a fade and made what I thought was a fade swing, a little more out-to-in than in-to-out through impact. I hooked anyway, my ball snagging the left rough, but I was in play.

And Henri took off.

The rascal didn't understand that caddies needed to exercise a great degree of decorum on such fine courses. Repair ball marks. Fix divots. Rake bunkers. Wipe the residue off of the clubs. Henri, by contrast, had a tendency to bark at the elk and chase down the stray snakes. But I was a clever owner, and a clever owner assimilates to the situation and uses it as a teaching moment. Each ball that I hit, and that Henri retrieved, merited one treat. If Henri left my ball in its original spot, that merited two treats. Henri was a quick study. After the first few slobber balls, Henri realized that if he simply stopped beside my ball and ceased his slobbering ways, he'd get not only two treats, but two very fancy ones. Out with the chicken and in with the venison. I knew how to play it, and Henri and I had been on the same page for most of the round. He was loving every second of it, and I was loving his companionship. A dog is man's best friend for a reason.

This time, Henri found my ball in twenty seconds. I took about twenty-five seconds with my cart. When I reached my ball, I looked at Henri, then back at my ball, then at the lie, then the flag, then at Henri again. If he was flustered, he didn't show it. He sat with his chest out and ears perked up, analyzing every sound known to man around him. He eventually gave up the act and started begging. I stared him down for a few seconds, and he went quiet. We were at a standstill. Then he held out his paw like a good citizen, and I took it.

"Good boy," I said.

Can't go wrong with venison. I handed him two more treats.

I had about three hundred and seven yards to the pin. Golf was the quintessential chess match. Position your ball at the right angles and quadrants, and you have a shot at shooting your best score. I wanted to lay up on the right side of the fairway, about one hundred fifty yards out. That would give me another one-hundred-fifty-yard shot to the green. Based on my ball striking today, that was a smooth seven iron. I took a couple practice swings and gave up my hooker card, at least for one shot. The ball faded this time, right to my landing spot.

Henri took off, and the process started again. Find ball. Drive cart. Staring contest. Give treat. Play on. When the round was over perhaps I'd go into the clubhouse and get some souvenirs for the road, to remember the place. Ever since I'd gotten out of Pontiac Correctional, I'd been the quintessential nomad. No car. No fixed address. No obligations. I'd gone from

Chicago to Oregon to Vegas to New Mexico, always with Henri by my side. I didn't feel comfortable in any one spot. And besides, I lived by my rules.

I had so much left to do with my second chance at life. When you come within seconds of receiving a government-sanctioned three-drug cocktail that will stop your heart forever, things become crystal clear. Next on the bucket list was Old Faithful in Yellowstone. Henri would get a kick out of the geothermal feature. Of course, this was all after I gave my speech tonight at Dobermans for Life. When word got out about how I'd rescued Henri, and the many talents he had developed on the trail, the society felt I'd be the perfect keynote speaker. I never turned down a good speech, and I'd accepted faster than a cheetah on the prowl.

But first, one more solid shot to go on eighteen. You're only as good as your next shot.

I surveyed the pin. It was tucked in the back left of the green, a few paces off the edge. A draw would get me there, but leave me with a big-ass sloping uphill putt. The safe play would be to hit to the fat part of the green, take my two putts, and call it a day. Even par for the back and that'd be all she wrote. The aggressive play would be to fly the ball right over the flag and have it check. If played absolutely perfectly, it'd check, hit the slope, and funnel back toward the hole.

Gravity.

I smiled and made the aggressive play. I took a nice divot, and dammit, I hit the perfect shot. My ball launched twenty degrees in the air and started drawing toward the flag. It landed two feet over the flag and checked. Then it started rolling down, closer and closer to perfection.

But then everything changed.

The ball hit something on the green and spun left. I still had a ten-footer for birdie, but I could have had a tap-in.

Henri was tired this time and hitched a ride in my cart. I drove all the way up to the cart path left of the green, parked, took my putter out, and walked to the obstruction that had messed with my shot. Normally I'd mark my ball, swat the obstruction aside, and get back to my putt.

Not now.

I froze.

The obstruction was a vintage Lord Marvel Seiko watch with the initials "R.S." engraved on the side of the crown.

It was my dad's watch.

The very same watch I'd seen buried at my mom's funeral.

GET The Loran Now on Amazon

JOIN GREG'S NEWSLETTER

For the latest updates on Greg's writing, sign up for his newsletter at: https://dashboard.mailerlite.com/forms/1415379/150624884207126495/share

ABOUT THE AUTHOR

Greg Gountanis writes mysteries and thrillers filled with a lot of action, wit, and courtroom drama. When he's not writing, he's lawyering. For over a decade, Greg's worked as a public defender in Chicago.

Get the latest news on Greg's books at www.greggountanis.com and on social media.

- **f** facebook.com/GregGountanisAuthor
- **a** amazon.com/stores/author/B08P1C58RR
- **▶** youtube.com/greggountanis

www.ingramcontent.com/pod-product-compliance
Lightning Source LLC
Chambersburg PA
CBHW032002240626
47153CB00003B/1088

9781953762016